Edwin D. Mead

A Memorial of John Greenleaf Whittier from His Native city,

Haverhill, Massachusetts

Edwin D. Mead

A Memorial of John Greenleaf Whittier from His Native city, Haverhill, Massachusetts

ISBN/EAN: 9783337328313

Printed in Europe, USA, Canada, Australia, Japan

Cover: Foto ©Raphael Reischuk / pixelio.de

More available books at **www.hansebooks.com**

A MEMORIAL

OF

John Greenleaf Whittier

FROM HIS NATIVE CITY

HAVERHILL

MASSACHUSETTS

" OH, NEVER MAY A SON OF THINE,
WHERE'ER HIS WANDERING STEPS INCLINE,
FORGET THE SKY WHICH BENT ABOVE
HIS CHILDHOOD LIKE A DREAM OF LOVE "

PUBLISHED BY AUTHORITY OF

The City Council

1893

CITY OF HAVERHILL, MASS.

In Common Council, *December* 29, 1892.

On motion of Councilman Lott F. McNamara,

Ordered, That the committee having in charge the recent services held in this city in honor of John Greenleaf Whittier be, and they hereby are, authorized with full powers to cause to be published a Memorial Volume containing an account of the same.

In Common Council, *December* 29, 1892.

Passed. Sent up,

Attest,

JESSE H. HARRIMAN,

Clerk.

In Board of Aldermen, *December* 29, 1892.

Concurred,   DAVID B. TENNEY,

City Clerk.

Approved, December 31, 1892.

THOMAS E. BURNHAM,

Mayor.

Owing to a lack of time to perform the duties assigned them before the expiration of their term of office, the members of this committee, on January 9, 1893, petitioned the succeeding City Council for the appointment of a new committee from their number to take up and perform the work with which they were charged, and the following action was taken : —

In Board of Aldermen, *January* 30, 1893.

On motion of Alderman Arthur E. Fernald,

Ordered, That a committee consisting of one Alderman and two Councilmen be appointed with full powers, to publish a memorial volume containing an account of the recent services held in this city in honor of John G. Whittier.

Passed and sent down. Alderman Fernald appointed.

Attest,

WILLIAM W. ROBERTS,

City Clerk.

In Common Council, *February* 8, 1893.

Passed in concurrence.

Councilmen Rufus C. Smith and Willard H. Hunkins appointed. Attest,

HORACE M. SARGENT,

Clerk.

Approved, February 15, 1893.

OLIVER TAYLOR,

Mayor.

At the first meeting of this committee, ex-President of the Board of Aldermen Charles W. Arnold and ex-Mayor Thomas E. Burnham were added to the committee and invited to assist in the work.

CONTENTS.

BIOGRAPHICAL SKETCH

THE

PUBL   A

JOHN GREENLEAF WHITTIER.

THE beloved poet, to whose memory this record of memorial services is fittingly consecrated, was born December 17, 1807, in the plain old farmhouse still standing in the eastern part of Haverhill, by the Amesbury road. Before him four generations of his ancestors, of the simple confidence, the plain life, and the pure spirituality of the Quaker faith, had lived in the same house, beginning with Thomas Whittier, who came from England in the good ship Confidence in 1638, and built this home about fifty years later. In the days of Indian warfare, the skulking savage on his murderous forays peered through its windows or pushed open its unbarred doors, but left unharmed its trustful occupants.

The father of John Greenleaf Whittier was John Whittier, a farmer in moderate circumstances, somewhat stern and dignified in carriage, a man of good ability and clear judgment. His mother was Abigail Hussey, a descendant of that Rev. William Bacheler of Hampton, N. H., who was the common ancestor of Whittier, Webster, Caleb Cushing and other distinguished men of New England, and

whose wonderful deep-set and expressive eyes re-
appeared as a striking physical characteristic in
his distinguished descendants. The other members of the family so exquisitely portrayed in
" Snow-Bound." were his sisters, Mary and Elizabeth, his brother, Mathew Franklin, his aunt,
Mercy Hussey, " the sweetest woman ever fate
perverse denied a household mate," and his father's brother, Moses, a gentle soul, innocent of
books but " rich in lore of fields and brooks." " In
the Whittier family," says his cousin, Gertrude
Cartland, " the reading of the Holy Scriptures was
a constant practice. On First-day afternoons,
especially, the mother would read them with the
children, endeavoring to impress their truths by
familiar conversation ; and to this early and habit-
ual instruction we may attribute in great measure
the full and accurate knowledge of Bible history
which the poems of John Greenleaf Whittier indicate, as well as the strong bias in favor of moral
reform which was so early manifested." The hos-
pitality of the home was ever extended to the
Quakers as they journeyed to their annual meetings, to the ministers of that faith, and to the best
society of a town that counted among its inhabi-
tants men of learning and of active participation
in all progressive movements. If for him who was
to immortalize the old house there was scant legacy
of gold and few books, there was the priceless in-
heritance of an ancestry of spiritual and earnest
habits of thought, the knowledge that fell fresh

from the lips of the thinker, and all about him the miracle of trees and flowers, the songs of birds, " green woods and moonlit snows." These things may not make a poet, but they may furnish subjects for his songs and form chords in them.

Born a farmer's boy, but physically delicate, fond of reading, but with few volumes to gratify his taste, Whittier was fourteen years old when Joshua Coffin, his first school-master, brought to his home a volume of Burns's poems, and left it for him to read. For him whose singularly pure soul sipped only the sweetness, the tender pathos and the humor from Burns's verse, the volume was a magic gift, breaking through the stern environment, and reaching to the fountains of song within him. Henceforth brook and flower sang to him, faith and aspiration were attuned to music, passion and indignation took the chords of the organ or the swelling tones of the trumpet. He was nineteen years old when his first poem, " The Exile's Departure," was printed in the " Free Press," a paper established in Newburyport, and having then as its editor a man destined not only to be a great influence in Whittier's life, but to be linked to him in soul and action against slavery — William Lloyd Garrison. Whittier tells very naïvely the story of this first published poem : " My father always had a weekly newspaper, and when young Garrison started his ' Free Press ' in Newburyport, he took it. My sister, who was two years older than myself, sent one of my poetical attempts to the editor. Some weeks afterward the news-carrier came along on horseback and threw the paper out from his saddle-bags. My uncle and I were mending fences. I took up the sheet, and was surprised and overjoyed to see my lines in the ' Poet's Corner.' I stood gazing at them in wonder, and my uncle had to call me several times to my work, before I could recover myself."

Without the knowledge of her brother, Mary Whittier had sent this poem to the "Free Press," which each week had published in its Poet's Corner some poem by Mrs. Hemans. These, Whittier's first published verses, were signed " W., Haverhill, June 1, 1826." Mr. Garrison describes as follows the manner in which the contribution came to him : " Going upstairs one day to my office, I observed a letter to my address lying near the door, which, on opening, I found to contain an original piece of poetry for my paper, written with very pale ink in a very fine hand. . . . As I was anxious to find out the writer, my post-rider divulged the secret, stating that he had dropped the letter in the manner described, and that it was written by a Quaker lad named Whittier, who was daily at work with hammer and lapstone at East Haverhill. Jumping into a vehicle, I lost no time in driving out to see the rustic bard, who came into the room with shrinking diffidence, almost unable to speak, and blushing like a maiden."

In this call Garrison not only encouraged Whittier and gave him honest praise, but he urged his father to give him a wider training. "Almost as soon as he could write," said Garrison in a later account of this first meeting, "Whittier gave evidence of the precocity and strength of his poetical genius, and when unable to procure paper and ink a piece of chalk or charcoal was substituted. He indulged his propensity for writing with so much secrecy that it was only by removing some rubbish in the garret that the discovery was made. The bent of his mind was discouraged by his parents. They were in indigent circumstances, and unable to give him a suitable education, and they did not wish to inspire him with hopes which might never be fulfilled. I endeavored to speak cheeringly of the prospects of their son. I dwelt upon the impolicy of warring against nature, of striving to quench the first kindlings of a flame that might burn like a star in our literary horizon, and I spoke of fame. 'Sir,' replied the father with an emotion that went home to my bosom, 'poetry will not give him bread.' The fate of Chatterton, Otway, and the whole catalogue of those who had perished by neglect rushed upon my memory and I was silent." Happily there was tougher fibre in the young poet than that whereof broken geniuses are made; there was the impulse to self-help, and the songs which came as the wind comes to the pine and the tide to the sea still found utterance. His hands wielded the hammer as well as the pen. He learned the art of making ladies' slippers, and in the following winter earned enough to procure a

suit of clothes and six months' tuition in the
Haverhill Academy, which opened that year. The
editor of the "Haverhill Gazette," Abijah Thayer,
used his influence in favor of the son's education. and on Mr. Thayer's promise to take him
into his own family, he was allowed to enter the
Academy. He was introduced to the preceptress,
Miss Arethusa Hall, who is still living (1893), as
"a young man who often, at the shoemaker's
bench, had hammered out fine verse." Miss Hall
describes him as at that time a tall, slight, distin-
guished-looking but bashful youth, with strikingly
beautiful eyes. After one term at the Haverhill
Academy. he became for a season the master of
the district school in the neighboring town of
Amesbury, and then returned to the Academy for
another six months of study. Meanwhile Garrison
had established in Boston the "National Philanthropist," and through his influence Whittier went
there, becoming a contributor to, and actually the
editor of "The American Manufacturer," a Boston
paper devoted to protection. The salary being
small and the home farm needing his help, he returned to Haverhill in June, 1829, and remained
a year; then in 1830 he edited for six months
"The Haverhill Gazette," doing his writing at his
father's home, and contributing to this and to other
papers many poems and prose-writings. In that
year George D. Prentice, the editor of "The New
England Weekly Review," published in Hartford,
Conn., went to Kentucky to write a life of Henry

Clay, and Whittier, who had been a frequent contributor to the Review, accepted the vacant position of editor, and filled it for a year and a half.

In 1832 he was again at home working, aided by his mother's economy and his sister's thrift, — for his father had died, — to make the old farm support the family, busy with literary work at such time as the farming allowed, and keeping up an active correspondence with Garrison, who, having with ceaseless activity attacked, now here and now there, the three great evils of slavery, war and intemperance, had at last, in Boston, a city which jeered him and heaped upon him every indignity, issued the first number of " The Liberator," containing the creed to which his heroic life was given : " Unconditional emancipation is the immediate duty of the master, and the immediate right of the slave." In the seclusion of his Haverhill home Whittier, pondering upon these things, gave the whole power of his genius to the service of Freedom. Thenceforward his verse became the mallet of Thor. It burned with holy wrath against wrong, it rebuked with holy hatred of evil, it stung the consciences of men into activity. But Whittier not only wrote; he acted. He befriended the English anti-slavery orator, George Thompson, and kept him in secret at his home two weeks. In Concord, N. H., he was mobbed with Thompson on the same night that Samuel J. May escaped from a mob in Haverhill by the friendly assistance of Whittier's sister, Elizabeth, and Harriet Minot.

2

Accompanying his sister to Boston, that she might attend the meetings of the Female Anti-Slavery Society, he saw the great mob that, seeking Thompson in vain, made Garrison its victim. In 1838 he became the editor of " The Pennsylvania Freeman," in Philadelphia. The office of the paper was sacked and burned by pro-slavery rioters, and shortly after Whittier returned to Massachusetts. In 1840 the home farm was sold, and the family removed to Amesbury to be nearer the Friends' meeting-house, and thenceforward for many years this was his home.

A constitution delicate from birth, and unequal to the demands of active life in crowded scenes, and a nature of which love of family, home, and familiar places was a strong attribute, made him henceforth what Longfellow affectionately called him, the " Hermit of Amesbury," and what Holmes gracefully named him, —

> " The wood-thrush of Essex, — you know whom I mean, —
> Whose song echoes round us while he sits unseen."

Perhaps from delicacy of health, perhaps from loyalty to the dear home circle, but certainly not from any disappointment, he deliberately put aside thoughts of marriage, and gave his affections, strong and unstinted, to his family and his friends. Unpopular for years because he was an abolitionist, he not only saw the triumph of the cause in which he struggled and was bruised, but he felt in his later years the swelling tribute of love and reverence from the North and South and East and West of

the purified and united land. When he had reached
the patriarchal age of full threescore and ten, "The
Atlantic Monthly" gave him a dinner, at which
the friends of his literary life in many a felicitous
address and poem uttered their affection and admiration. His response to their greetings and tributes
was read by Longfellow : —

> " Beside that milestone where the level sun,
> Nigh unto setting, sheds his last, low rays
> On word and work irrevocably done,
> Life's blending threads of good and ill outspun,
> I hear, O friends ! your words of cheer and praise,
> Half doubtful if myself or otherwise,
> Like him who in the old Arabian joke
> A beggar slept and crowned caliph woke.
> Thanks not the less. With not unglad surprise
> I see my life-work through your partial eyes ;
> Assured in giving to my home-taught songs
> A higher value than of right belongs,
> You do but read between the written lines
> The finer grace of unfulfilled designs."

Thereafter, though he lived not so long as
Holmes wished, —

> " Till we 've paid him in love half the balance we owe," —

for fourteen years each succeeding birthday was a
festival of love-giving from his friends.

On his last birthday on earth, his friends who
dwell at Haverhill made a call upon him at the
home of his cousins, the Cartlands, in Newburyport. As he came to meet them he spoke his
love in kindly words of greeting and added, mod-
estly : " It cannot be said of me that I am a prophet without honor save in my own house, for I

have ever been signally honored by my dear towns-
people." The memory of him that bright winter
morning, as he entered the room where flowers and
gifts and fond messages from absent friends beto-
kened wide love and dear remembrance, is effface-
able. His spare form, tall and erect, the lofty dome
of thought crowned with thin, whitened locks, the
deep-set and lustrous eyes, the gentle mien, the
warm but simple greeting — formed a picture of
age not decrepit, but fragile and spiritualized.

A few months later, September 7, 1892, at day-
break, he died. The summer, which he termed
one of the happiest of his life, had been spent at
Hampton Falls, in the home of his dear friend, Miss
Gove. This parish had been the home of his
mother's people, of the Rev. Stephen Bacheler
and Christopher Hussey, and the home was that
wherein his friend's mother and his mother's friend,
Mrs. Gove, an eloquent preacher, had lived and
died. It was of her that he sang so tenderly in
" The Friend's Burial " (1873) : —

> " My thoughts are all in yonder town,
>   Where, wept by many tears,
>   To-day my mother's friend lays down
>   The burden of her years.
>
>   .   .   .   .   .   .
>
> " The dear Lord's best interpreters
>   Are humble human souls;
>   The gospel of a life like hers
>   Is more than books or scrolls."

On the Saturday following his transition, in
the garden of his former home at Amesbury, the
friends of his earlier and his later days gathered for

the last reverential service, "after the manner of the Friends," as he had willed it. There were the few remaining of those who, with him, had "uplifted the ark of liberty," comrades of the authors' guild, neighbors and friends, "dear memories in each mourner's heart, like heaven's white lilies." And after the touching service they left him at sundown in the "Friends' Lot," whither all of his father's family had preceded him, the ferns shielding his coffin from the clay, and the closely heaped flowers spreading their perfume like incense above him.

ALBERT LE ROY BARTLETT.

THE CITY'S TRIBUTE.

THE CITY'S TRIBUTE.

THE passing away of Mr. Whittier was not an unexpected event; for days the people of Haverhill had waited with sad and anxious hearts for the latest tidings from his bedside. The slender thread that bound his pure soul to earth was still bearing the strain; but yet its tender strands, as one by one they yielded, announced like the ticking of a clock that the hour was at hand, and that the spirit that had fluttered on the border land was about to yield to the inevitable summons.

On the announcement of his death, the flags of the city were immediately placed at half-mast and the citizens were acquainted with the sad tidings by tolling eighty-five strokes upon the City Hall bell, and the following proclamation of His Honor the Mayor: —

CITY OF HAVERHILL,
EXECUTIVE DEPARTMENT, CITY HALL,
September 7, 1892.

To THE CITIZENS OF HAVERHILL : With feelings of unfeigned sorrow the people of our city will receive the sad intelligence of the death at Hampton Falls, N. H., of Haverhill's most illustrious son, JOHN GREENLEAF WHITTIER.

It would be idle at this time to attempt to recount his labors or to describe his achievements. As a man of letters the world bears record of his fame. His genius was unexcelled. His purity of thought and life, his compassion for the unfortunate, and his heart that was ever open for his kind, stamp him as one who will receive the honor and homage of every nation and every tongue.

But to us, the people of the city that gave him birth, there is a still tenderer tie. It was here that he spent his childhood and received his early inspiration : here he wrought in the same industries by which we earn our daily bread. Our hills, our woods, our lakes and our traditions furnished themes for his gifted pen. Nay, we have felt the strength of his citizenship and the warmth of his love, and it is with peculiar and heartfelt sorrow that we mourn for our own.

In token of this sorrow, the house in which he was born will be appropriately draped in mourning ; the flags upon the public buildings will remain at half-mast until after the obsequies ; the bells upon the City Hall and churches will be tolled, and the city offices will be closed during the funeral hour ; at that time the teachers in the public schools will lay aside all other duties and cause appropriate mention to be made of his character and works, — that our citizens may give proper expression to the universal lament.

THOMAS E. BURNHAM,
Mayor.

In addition to these manifestations of sorrow, others both of a public and private nature were apparent alike at the hearthstone, the workshop, and the trading place. Copious and creditable mention of his character and worth was made by the press of the city, private residences and places of business on every hand bore insignia of sorrow, and the whole people mourned for him as for a beloved friend.

The City Council and city officials attended his funeral at Amesbury in a body, and, following his remains to their last resting-place, joined with those near and dear to him in casting their tributes of love and affection upon his bier.

At an appropriate time the City Council enacted the following: —

CITY OF HAVERHILL, *September* 15, 1892.

A special meeting of the City Council was held at 7.30 o'clock P. M., in accordance with the request of the mayor, His Honor Mayor BURNHAM in the chair.

The mayor called attention of the Council to the recent death of our distinguished fellow-citizen JOHN GREENLEAF WHITTIER, and paid a fitting tribute to his patriotism, his genius, and his exemplary life.

CHARLES W. ARNOLD, Chairman of the Board of Aldermen, and President ANDREW E. FAY of the Common Council, also made appropriate remarks in relation to the same.

Alderman CHARLES W. ARNOLD introduced the following: —

"In the death of JOHN GREENLEAF WHITTIER the nation has lost an ardent and conscientious patriot; those who knew him best are deprived of the counsel and sympathy of an earnest and faithful friend, and the world of letters mourns for him as one of her most gifted sons; but far above all this, humanity has lost a friend.

" The earliest and best years of his life, the brilliancy of his youth and the vigor of his manhood were devoted, with an unsparing zeal and with all the energy of his soul, to the cause of the down-trodden and the oppressed.

" No sweeter songs than his ever told the legends and traditions of New England, or with more delightful phrase set forth the charm and beauties of our native land; and no other pen has ever been more fearless than his in denouncing wrong and contending for the right.

" His life has been pure, spotless, unblemished, ' without fear and without reproach.'

" As representatives of his birthplace and of the home he loved so well, we offer this tribute to his memory. And while we deeply lament his loss, we are thankful to the Giver of every good and perfect gift that for a period far beyond the allotted time his life was spared; that his last years were peaceful and happy; and that of him it can be truly said : —

> " ' None knew him but to love him,
> None named him but to praise.' "

Adopted unanimously by a rising vote, and ordered to be entered in full on the city records.

Attest,

DAVID B. TENNEY,
City Clerk.

In BOARD OF ALDERMEN, *September* 15, 1892.

On motion of Alderman ARTHUR E. FERNALD,

Ordered, That a committee consisting of His Honor the Mayor, two members of the Board of Aldermen, the President and two members of the Common Council, be appointed with full powers to make all necessary arrangements for a memorial service in honor of Haverhill's distinguished and lamented son, JOHN GREENLEAF WHITTIER.

Passed unanimously.

Aldermen ARTHUR E. FERNALD and CHARLES W. AR-NOLD appointed on committee.

Attest,

DAVID B. TENNEY,
City Clerk.

IN COMMON COUNCIL, *September* 15, 1892.

Concurred unanimously by a rising vote.

In addition to President ANDREW E. FAY, Councilmen LOTT F. McNAMARA and HARRY E. BEAN were ap-pointed. Attest,

JEROME S. FULLER,
Clerk pro tem.

MEMORIAL SERVICES.

The City Council of Haverhill
respectfully invite you to attend the Memorial
Services in honor of her distinguished Son
John Greenleaf Whittier.
to be held at City Hall, December 21st 1892.
The eulogy will be pronounced by
Thomas Wentworth Higginson.
The services will begin at Two thirty o'clock precisely.

Thomas E. Burnham, Chairman

Charles W. Arnold,   Harry E. Bean.

Andrew E. Fay,   Lott F. McNamara.

Arthur E. Fernald.

Committee of Arrangements.

AE
TIL

MEMORIAL SERVICES.

WITH true maternal pride the people of Haverhill had
watched the career of their gifted son; and as step by step he
climbed the ladder of fame, they felt that, while he was winning
for himself the grateful homage of the world, he was adding
honor and glory to the good name of his native city. Their
fair fields had been rendered fairer, the blue waters of their
lakes clearer, and the cool shade of their trees and woods
more refreshing. The grandeur of their hills had an added
charm, and the merry ripple of their brooks and streams sounded
sweeter, because of them he had sung, and because all had been
to him "sweet promptings unto kindest deeds;" and now that
he was gone, they felt that, in proper form, their homage was
his due.

> " Let laurels drenched in pure Parnassian dews,
> Reward his memory, dear to every muse,
> Who with a courage of unshaken root,
> In honor's field advancing his firm foot,
> Plants it upon the line that Justice draws,
> And will prevail, or perish in her cause.
> 'T is to the virtues of such men man owes
> His portion in the good that Heaven bestows."

Obedient, therefore, to this sentiment, and in accordance with
the wish of the City Council, as expressed in the foregoing order, arrangements were made for a suitable commemorative
service to be held in City Hall on Wednesday, December 21,
1892. Invitations were issued to distinguished literary, philan-
thropic, political, religious, and personal friends of Mr. WHIT-
TIER to be present and participate in the services, for which
the following order of exercises had been arranged : —

3

MEMORIAL SERVICE

IN HONOR OF

JOHN GREENLEAF WHITTIER.

BY THE CITY COUNCIL,

CITY HALL,

December twenty-first, at 2.30 P. M.,

1892.

COMMITTEE OF ARRANGEMENTS:

THOMAS E. BURNHAM, Chairman.

CHARLES W. ARNOLD,   HARRY E. BEAN,

ANDREW E. FAY.   LOTT F. McNAMARA.

ARTHUR E. FERNALD.

ORDER OF EXERCISES.

INTRODUCTION,   .   . .   *THE MAYOR.*

PRAYER, .   .   .   *REV. EDWARD EVERETT HALE.*

SINGING, .   .   .   *. PHILHARMONIC QUARTETTE.*

"Thy Will Be Done,"— John Greenleaf Whittier.

POEM, ...   *. WILL CARLETON.*

SINGING, .   .   .   *. PHILHARMONIC QUARTETTE.*

"My Birthday,"— Whittier.

EULOGY, .   .   *. THOMAS WENTWORTH HIGGINSON.*

"The singer of a farewell rhyme,
Upon whose utmost verge of time,
The shades of night are falling down,
I pray God bless the good old town."

SINGING, .   .   .   *. PHILHARMONIC QUARTETTE.*

"Auld Lang Syne."

After the arrangement of this programme, the committee were obliged to supply the places of Rev. EDWARD EVERETT HALE, who had been selected to offer the opening prayer, and Col. THOMAS WENTWORTH HIGGINSON, who was to deliver the eulogy. Both of these gentlemen had accepted the committee's invitation, but later, being unable to be present, were obliged to decline, the latter in consequence of ill-health. They were. however, very ably succeeded by the Rev. GEORGE H. REED, pastor of the North Congregational Church, in place of Mr. HALE ; and Mr. EDWIN D. MEAD, editor of the " New England Magazine." in place of Colonel HIGGINSON.

The City Hall had been tastefully arranged for the occasion, and decorated with rare plants, ferns, and flowers. A life-size portrait of the great poet, and a fine engraving of his birthplace, rested upon easels at either end of the stage, that had been materially enlarged to accommodate the large and distinguished company of invited guests.

This company constituted a rare gathering, and one long to be remembered. Besides the official guests, those who lent the dignity of their personal or official presence as the representatives of the nation, the state, the county, the city of his nativity, and the town of his adoption, there were also his kindred, his neighbors, the poet, the writer, the reformer, the venerable anti-slavery advocate, as well as the plain-garbed devotee of his religious faith, and those with whom he had labored in every good work to which he had set his hand, and, last but not least, those near and dear personal friends who had felt the vigor of his friendship and the warmth of his love.

At 2.15 o'clock P. M., there assembled at the City Council rooms the city officials and invited guests, who proceeded in a body to the hall, occupying seats that had been reserved for them, after escorting the distinguished guests and those who were to participate in the exercises to the platform. The procession moved in the following order under the direction of the City Messenger : —

The President and Members of the Common Council.
The President and Members of the Board of Aldermen.
The Mayor.   The Chaplain.
The Poet.   The Eulogist.
The ex-Mayors.
The Quartette.
The City Officials and Heads of Departments.
Senators and Representatives in the General Court.
County Officials.
The School Board.
The Board of Assessors.
The Board of Overseers of the Poor.
The Board of Health.
The Commissioners of Sinking Funds.
The Trustees of the Public Library.
The Board of Registrars of Voters.
The Trustees of the City Hospital.
The Park Commission.
The Water Board.
The Whittier Club.
And other invited guests.

The entire seating capacity of the hall was filled with an intelligent, appreciative, and cultured audience. Promptly at 2.30 o'clock the exercises proceeded as follows. His Honor Mayor Thomas E. Burnham, introducing the same, said: —

Ladies and Gentlemen, — The sacred purpose for which we meet to-day might well call together the people of any community in the civilized world.

To honor the memory of the great, the wise, and the good by suitable expression has at all times and under all conditions of civilization been a criterion by which to judge of the degree of intelligence, morality, and refinement attained. In their ideals we may measure their aspirations and ambitions.

If the good man whose memory we attempt to-day to honor was dear to the world; if others found in his life, in his gifted pen, in his noble thoughts, and in his good deeds that which endeared him to their hearts and strengthened their lives, — is it not fitting that we, who would not draw him from the great pedestal of his world-wide fame, but with all the devotion that the ties of kindred and the seal of birthright can give, should pay our tribute to the memory of our own?

What he was to the world he was to us; but we knew him as the world did not. Here he was born. Here he spent his childhood. At our public schools was he taught. By our simple industries did he live, and by our themes was he inspired. For us were written the thoughts of his early life, and to us alone was accorded the privilege of constituting him our representative in legislative halls. It is therefore fitting that we, of all the world, should honor ourselves by paying our loving tribute to his memory.

Therefore, obedient to the will of the citizens of Haverhill, as expressed by the City Council, let us in these exercises render due homage to his name and worth, first rendering thanks to the Giver of all good for all that he has wrought, and that it was our privilege to be so closely allied to his noble life.

The Rev. George H. Reed, pastor of the North Church, gave devout thanks, and invoked the divine blessing in the following words: —

We thank Thee, our heavenly Father, that in a city preëminent for its devotion to business, this audience is assembled to honor the memory of one the aim of whose life was higher than the ambition to accumulate wealth. Here may we be reminded that man is most honored, not by that which a city may do for him, but by that which he has done for the city.

Impress upon us, we pray Thee, the close connection between our characters and the character of our city. May we hear him who, being dead, yet speaketh, saying again to us : —

> " The riches of the Commonwealth
> Are free, strong minds, and hearts of health ;
> And more to her than gold or grain
> The cunning hand and cultured brain."

We thank Thee, O God, for the mental endowment which enabled our beloved poet to eliminate from the ordinary events of life that which is incidental and temporary, and to reveal to our dull sight the eternal, essential, and universal truth. We are thankful that he has interpreted Nature to us, and taught us to appreciate our lakes, our rivers, and our hills. We thank Thee that he has also revealed to us the beauty of common things, teaching us to call nothing commonplace which signifies fidelity and conscientious effort.

His words have been to us like apples of gold in pictures of silver, and his thoughts as doves with wings of silver and feathers covered with yellow gold. In him Thou hast fulfilled the promise that a man shall be as an hiding-place from the wind, and as the shadow of a great rock in a weary land.

There are many precious memories and impressive lessons of which we would make mention before Thee, O God, as here in the city of his birth and boyhood we meet to pay our homage to the memory of our friend. We pray that the happy combination of courage and of mildness which we admired in him may make us at once lowly in spirit and loyal to freedom and to duty. And we are reminded by the thought of his spirit that his desire would be that in our prayer we should praise Thee rather than him for all the hope and light and help he gave to men.

And now, O God, Thou knowest more of all our needs than all our prayers have told. We only bow in lowliness of mind before thy throne, and pray for grace to know and to do thy will. This, and all things else for which we ought to pray, we ask in the name and the merits of Him who is the Lord and Master of us all. Amen.

Following the invocation the Philharmonic Quartette, Messrs. CHARLES F. MORRISON, WILLIAM E. HARTWELL, ARTHUR T. JACOBS, and HENRY S. SPRAGUE, sang in an impressive manner the great poet's " Thy Will Be Done," the music for which was composed by City Clerk DAVID B. TENNEY.

THY WILL BE DONE.

We see not, know not; all our way
Is night, — with thee alone is day;
From out the torrent's troubled drift,
Above the storm our prayers we lift,
    Thy will be done !

Though dim as yet in tint and line,
We trace thy picture's wise design,
And thank thee that our age supplies
Its dark relief of sacrifice.
        Thy will be done!

And if, in our unworthiness,
The sacrificial wine we press;
If from thy ordeal's heated bars
Our feet are seamed with crimson scars,
        Thy will be done!

Strike, thou the Master, we thy keys,
The anthem of the destinies!
The minor of thy loftier strain,
Our hearts shall breathe the old refrain,
        Thy will be done!

Mayor BURNHAM then said: —

There are those whom we would gladly greet to-day to share with us the pleasures of this tribute. But while we cannot welcome them in person, we shall not be denied their good words, and I will ask Mr. ALBERT L. BARTLETT to respond for our absent friends.

Mr. BARTLETT's response was as follows: —

To remember the absent, Mr. Chairman, is one of the tenderest characteristics of mankind. The unseen guests sit at all our festivals; they are present at all our memorials. Their hands clasp ours, their voices are heard in our hearts, their memory abides there.

But I am not here to speak in words of my own for those who are absent, but to read from those

whom distance, illness, or other engagements keep
away, their own messages of regret, and, first of
all, that of His Excellency the Governor of the
Commonwealth : —

COMMONWEALTH OF MASSACHUSETTS.

EXECUTIVE DEPARTMENT.

BOSTON, *December* 16, 1892.

HON. THOMAS E. BURNHAM, *Haverhill, Mass.*

MY DEAR SIR. — I regret extremely to be obliged to decline
the invitation of the City Council of Haverhill to attend the
memorial services in honor of her distinguished son, Mr. Whittier, on December 21.

I am greatly disappointed to find that on that day I have
an imperative official engagement which makes it impossible
for me to accept the invitation. I am sure that your distinguished orator, Mr. Higginson, who was so closely in sympathy
with Mr. Whittier in his beliefs, his work, and his tastes, will
most ably and eloquently set forth the great services Whittier
has rendered to our people and the country as well as to literature and learning.

Very truly yours,

WM. E. RUSSELL.

137 WEST 78TH ST., NEW YORK,
December 17, 1892.

HON. THOMAS E. BURNHAM, *Chairman of the Memorial
Committee. Haverhill, Mass.*

DEAR SIR, — With thanks for the remembrance, I acknowledge the invitation of your City Council to attend the memorial
services of the 21st inst. in honor of John Greenleaf Whittier.

It is a matter of sincere regret on my part that I cannot then
be present to hear the oration, and to join in your affectionate
tribute to the dearest and most national of our elder poets. The
recollection of my associations with Mr. Whittier is to me one of
the most precious things of life. I loved him, — and who did

not that knew him? And who did not feel that they knew him, knowing his life and works? I shared your veneration for him as a man, your admiration of his song, matchless in its native quality, its tenderness, its noble wrath, its sacred aspiration.

His name and fame will last. They are a shining, inseparable part of the American story, of the American sentiment at its most exalted height. *

Very truly yours,

Edmund C. Stedman.

Chicago, Ill., *December* 20, 1892.

Hon. Thomas E. Burnham.

Dear Sir, — It would be to me a great pleasure to participate in the ceremonies in honor of the late John Greenleaf Whittier on the 21st of December. But the fact of my being a thousand miles distant from Haverhill at the time of receiving the notice (and the notice itself being delayed by the mails until the 19th) precluded the possibility.

I am the more interested in Mr. Whittier on account of my personal acquaintance with him, and occasional delightful visits to him in his summer home at Oak Knoll. My wife also was a schoolmate with him in the Haverhill Academy in his youth, and is now almost the only survivor of those who were associated with him in his early studies. In common with the whole English-speaking world, I venerate and admire this poet of New England life, and especially as the poet of human nature and of the heart. While he was a Quaker by profession, he never swerved from his ancestral faith. Amid the new surroundings and temptations of his manhood, he was never ashamed of the gospel as he understood it. At the same time he was a reverential and devout Christian, independently of all distinctive creeds. His heart was ever alive to the needs and the trials of human nature. He was the friend of every sufferer, and the advocate of all the down-trodden and oppressed. Never swayed by ambition for popularity or personal ease, he sacrificed himself on the altar of benevolence, that he might speak for the dumb, and deliver the victims of injustice and wrong. That

noble heart throbbed only in harmony with the just, the true,
and the good. A true son of New England, he delighted in
its institutions, and was never more happy than when he portrayed its history, its customs, its pursuits, and its joys.

It was his rare good fortune through a Divine Providence to
survive to a good old age. when the excitements of a busy life
were past ; when the false judgments under which he had suf-
fered were corrected ; when his enemies were transformed into
friends and admirers, and all the literary and loving world were
glad to do him honor.

His latest poems, fitting finale of a fragrant spring and summer career, breathe a beautiful spirit of Christian faith. They
are a charming swan song, with which to close so rare a life.
Never were sweeter words written by poet of any age or nation
than those in one of his latest productions : —

> " I know not where his islands lift
>   Their fronded palms in air ;
> I only know I cannot drift
>   Beyond God's loving care."

And the closing stanzas of his last poem, addressed to Dr. Oliver
Wendell Holmes on his birthday, were as beautiful as if his lips
had already been touched by the live coal of the seraph from
the heavenly altar, that he might finish his work on earth, by
anticipation, with the song of the angels.

God be thanked that such a life was lived, and that it was so
prolonged. Its rich influence will continue to unfold in blessings for generations yet unborn.

Faithfully yours,

S. F. SMITH.

HARTFORD, *December* 19, 1892.

MR. BURNHAM : DEAR SIR, — I thank the gentlemen of
the City Council of Haverhill for their polite kindness in sending me an invitation to be present at the memorial services to
be held in their city, December 21, in honor of Mr. Whittier, a
man dear to the heart of the whole nation, and doubly dear to
the New England heart. I regret that I am not able to attend.

It would be very interesting to hear the eulogy on that occasion given by another of the brave band who dared to act for right and justice when it took courage to do so.

Sincerely yours,
HARRIET BEECHER STOWE.

EXETER, N. H., *December* 21, 1892.

To THOMAS E. BURNHAM, *and others, Committee of Arrangements.*

GENTLEMEN, — Please accept my thanks for the honor conferred by your invitation to be present at the memorial services for Whittier. I regret that duties in another direction prevent my attendance. Your energetic city honors itself in honoring the memory of him who is at once the poet-seer of the human conscience and the sweet bard of New England life and scenes. If less gifted than Burns, he far surpasses that glorious Scottish bard by the nobleness of his life and the purity of his verse. "The Cotter's Saturday Night" and "Snow-Bound" are twin idyls that may well lie beside the Bible and hymn-book in the homes of New England. No policy dictated Whittier's conscience. No church, no prophet, no history of wrong conduct even in the most sacred of books, could lead his conscience, or induce him to disobey that "inner light," — his sensitive and enlightened conscience, that voice of God in his soul. If the chaste Joseph enslaved the starving sons of Egypt, or the sainted Paul sent a man back to slavery, Whittier saw no reason why he should drive hard bargains with necessitous men, or return men to slavery. He felt himself responsible to his heavenly Father, not for the actions of Joseph or Paul, but for those of John G. Whittier.

Haverhill is fortunate for having in its heroic youth been the home of such a heroine as Mrs. Dustin, and in its later years the birthplace of the poet of the people. The little, old-time persecuted sect, and in recent times almost forgotten people, the Friends or Quakers, are singularly fortunate in having given to New England the poet Whittier, and to Old England the orator and statesman, John Bright, — two among the very best and noblest of the historical characters of the nineteenth century.

Very truly,

J. D. Lyman.

Boston, *December* 19, 1892.

Hon. Thomas E. Burnham, *Chairman.*

Dear Sir, — I am highly honored in being invited by the City Council of Haverhill to attend their memorial service on the 21st inst. I would gladly unite in any tribute to her eminent son, John Greenleaf Whittier. He deserves more than can be paid him. Accept my grateful acknowledgments, with my sincere regrets that age and ill-health must keep me at home.

Yours respectfully and truly,

Robert C. Winthrop.

There are other brief letters of regret, from which I need not read.[1]

I have placed last in this series of letters the regrets and tribute of one who was for a while a resident of Haverhill, and who has borne with him in his high ministry elsewhere the love of those who were taught and inspired by him here : —

---

[1] Letters were received from Hon. Henry L. Dawes, Hon. Henry Cabot Lodge, Gen. William Cogswell, Hon. William C. Endicott, Hon. A. E. Pillsbury, Hon. A. S. Pinkerton, Hon. W. W. Rice, H. O. Houghton, Esq., Mrs. Elizabeth Stuart Phelps Ward, Mrs. Celia Thaxter, Miss Edna Dean Proctor, Mrs. Ednah D. Cheney, Miss Katherine E. Conway, Horace E. Scudder, Esq., Charles Dudley Warner, Esq., Rev. D. T. Fiske, President C. W. Eliot of Harvard University, William Hale, Esq., Hon. Charles Theodore Russell, M. M. Fisher, Esq., Mayor Asa G. Andrews, of Gloucester, Daniel Gurteen, Jr., Executive of Haverhill, England, and F. B. Sanborn, Esq.

NEW HAVEN, CONN., *December* 19, 1892.

MR. THOMAS E. BURNHAM, *Chairman of Committee of Arrangements.*

MY DEAR SIR, — I have the honor to acknowledge the receipt of an invitation to attend the services in memory of John Greenleaf Whittier to be held in Haverhill on the 21st of December.

It would give me great pleasure to join in these services if my professional duties would allow me to do so.

In ancient days, a city sometimes adopted a patron saint in the belief that he would bring help and deliverance in times of danger.

The superstition needs to be but slightly altered to become of use in these days. A patron saint, if rightly chosen and truly honored, may still deliver a city from its gravest evils.

If, in days to come, Haverhill should yield to the spirit of mere "getting and spending;" if it should forget its duty to the nation; if it should become faithless to humanity and to God, — it will only need to remember Whittier to find deliverance from these dangers.

May I be permitted to express as a sentiment appropriate to the occasion, —

John Greenleaf Whittier: Poet, Philanthropist, Teacher, the Patron Saint of Haverhill.

Very truly yours,

T. T. MUNGER.

There is another friend, absent from us to-day, whose heart and thoughts, I doubt not, turn to this assemblage. I have from him no words of regret. His message came last evening to the Whittier Club in the form of a deed conveying to trustees chosen from that society the genius-hallowed old farmhouse and the surrounding acres known as the Whittier Birthplace.

Under the wise care of these trustees, restored to its old-time appearance, the old, familiar articles, the bull's-eye watch that hung in view, the and-irons' glow, the motley-braided mat, and even the old gray wizard's conjuring book, each in its wonted place, this historic place will be our heritage and the heritage of all future generations, its doors open to all who come with reverent feet. While we remember the dead, let us pause a moment to give gratitude to the living, the generous donor, the Hon. JAMES H. CARLETON.

The mayor then introduced the poet in the following words : —

As a reformer, as a teacher, as a scholar, as a philosopher, as a wise counselor, and as a faithful friend, the name of Whittier will live on through the ages so long as the English tongue shall be spoken or the American name be known. But that which will engrave his name upon the hearts of all future generations, and cause him to be remembered should all else fail, will be the sweet songs he has sung, clothing in language pure and chaste the principles of right. And to-day I present you one skilled to weave in melody his own pure thoughts, and well worthy to pay our tribute in kind to our honored dead.

I introduce WILL CARLETON, of Brooklyn, New York.

Mr. CARLETON then read in an effective and scholarly manner his " Ode to Whittier."

ODE TO WHITTIER.

I.

If Industry, Humanity, and Truth
Have laid the solid stepping-stones of Youth,
If they have smiled upon a Summer-time,
And strewed with flowers the pathway of a prime,
If tenderly they have bent down and kissed
A toil-worn brow amid the Autumn mist,
If they have decked, with e'er-increasing glow,
Unsullied drifts of Manhood's purest snow,
If every action Memory leads to mind
Has been a free help-offering to mankind,
Until the good man's very form and face
Becomes a benediction to his race, —
    Then let the world take cheer ;
But when within that life of goodly fame
Creeps Genius, with its ne'er-extinguished flame,
Till every thought reverberates afar,
And every word throws radiance like a star,
And Honor's torch lights up its every hour,
And the whole world admits a master's power,
When every moon has listened, fondly long,
To the sweet cadence of another song,
And each sun's golden finger has thrown bare
The mighty thoughts that made their ambush there, —
    Then reverence must appear ;
Then the proud earth its wrinkled hand must raise,
And crown the singer with its choicest bays ;
And so, to-day, we ask the world to praise
    Our good and grand Whittier !

II.

Sing, Merrimac ! lift thy sweet voice above
All other streams ; thou wast his river-love !
  4

Through thy green valleys crept the unclad feet
That soon should walk Fame's palace-bordered street;
Upon thy banks first flashed the dreams in view,
That brightened all the world in coming true;
He loved the gallant words and deeds to praise
Of thy advance-guard of Colonial days;
He loved upon Fame's canvas high to lift
Thy brilliant present, with its scenes of thrift;
He strove to make thy future doubly sure,
With precepts, which like diamonds will endure;
    His spirit lingers here!
Thou wast his teacher: from thy lips he learned
Lessons that lesser men had lost or spurned:
As thou couldst smile at sky and cloud and tree,
And pave with song thy pathway to the sea,
And still couldst pause, in needful time and place,
To toil and struggle for the human race,
So he could court the zephyr or the flower
That helped to pass a sweetly idle hour,
Then fly away from pleasures, when he ought,
To turn the massive enginery of thought,
    For bringing Heaven more near!
So this, O river, let thy burden be,
And sing it from the mountain to the sea;
There was no grander man on earth than he —
    The sweet — the strong Whittier!

III.

You mountains, write his name, in letters high,
Upon the tinted pages of the sky!
He used upon thy granite roofs to stand,
And fondly gaze across his Fatherland;
To trace the checkered cloaks, in shifting crowds,
Thrown o'er thee by the shadows of the clouds;
To see the kingly battles of the storms,
That raved around thy staid and stately forms;
Or read the sun's midwinter message bright
Flashing upon thy signal towers of white.

Thou wert but stations toward his shining goal;
For in his lofty heart, and mind, and soul,
    He was a mountaineer!
Boast of him, mountains, for he learned of thee;
He saw the clouds come sweeping from the sea,
He saw thee prisoned in their midday gloom,
And buried deep within a vapor-tomb;
And still imagined that thou couldst descry
That all was well, and wait there for the sky!
When joys of earth were shrouded from our view,
He told us Heaven would soon come smiling through;
When our sad nation delved in deepest night,
To his pure spirit, God was still in sight;
    He saw the promise clear.
Look upward, mountains! he has onward passed;
But his great shadow o'er the cliffs is cast,
And long among thy peaks his name shall last —
    The lofty-souled Whittier!

IV.

Tell of him, Ocean; let thy cold waves be
Each one a voice; he loved to sing of thee.
He traced thy tossing pathways o'er and o'er —
He mourned the wrecks that lashed thy wailing shore;
Full oft he made thy guests once more engage
In dramas on thy great cloud-curtained stage:
He camped with thee, thy legends sweetly sung,
Now heard where'er the heart has found a tongue;
He sought thy shore for Sea-dreams, sadly true,
Of the sweet girl-love that his boyhood knew.
Thou wast his teacher, ancient, gray-haired sea;
His lofty genius lessons learned from thee,
    Its steadfast course to steer;
For thou each day art sending, one by one,
Thy foaming billows upward toward the sun,
Which, marshalled in their cloud-flotillas grand,
Sail o'er the harvest field and desert-land,
Then cast to earth their glittering, life-charged seeds,
And minister once more to mortal needs.

And this man's genius, soaring toward the sky,
Flashed in the sunlight, pleased the gazing eye,
Then, with obedient furtherance of God's plan,
Sought earth again. to minister to man,
    Fresh. fragrant deeds to rear ;
So. Ocean. now a deep-voiced song from thee ;
And let its many-octaved burden be,
His heart was deep and boundless as the sea —
    The mighty-souled Whittier !

V.

O Summer, when again thou claim'st the hours,
Write on his grave an epitaph of flowers.
See that the pansy's gentle face has brought
Its messages of sweet and pleasant thought ;
Let the pure lily come, with aspect meek.
And violets his modesty bespeak :
Make rosebuds symbolize an unknown name,
Then blossom forth, as did his fragrant fame ;
With thy persuasive touch, guide to the spot
The kind and starry-eyed forget-me-not ;
Let every flower with honor in its bloom,
Aid to adorn that low but lofty tomb —
    That never-hidden bier !
Unpicked bouquets for his free spirit blow,
Even where the hidden forest-gardens grow :
Each blossom must a perfumed message send
To him, at once its lover and its friend ;
Each true-voiced bird must linger o'er him long,
And give the sleeping master song for song ;
Each moon-ray pierce, with radiance dreamy-bright,
The soft sad stillness of the summer night,
And every morning sun more keenly shine,
To guide some pilgrim to that honored shrine,
    With reverent words sincere ;
Sing of him, Summer ! set thy zephyrs free ;
Let the true song float over hill and lea,
No sweeter spirit lived on earth than he —
    The gentle-faced Whittier !

VI.

O Winter, that upon the earth hast thrown
White dazzling fields and hilltops of thine own,
When the trim cottage chimney flings in sight
'Gainst thy clear sky its shivering breath of white,
When children of the fountains and the rains
Peer upward through thy frosted window-panes,
When gardens grow the ice-flowers on their stems,
And trees are open caskets full of gems,
Or when the muffled earth can hear and feel
Thy frozen storm-cloud's lengthened thunder-peal,
Disturb not then the poet's peaceful rest ;
Plant lightly thy white footsteps on his breast ;
     He loved thy splendors drear ;
Each twelvemonth to his calm, kind nature lent
Not sorrow, but a winter of content ;
Each gave new time to comfort and to bless ;
His birthdays were not signals of distress.
Each saw wide banners of his love unfurled,
Each brought new greetings from a grateful world.
Though arctic blasts might compass him around,
His radiant heart was never once " snow-bound ; "
He always singing paced his foot-worn way,
And even " at sundown " of a winter day,
     Through past joys he would peer.
Winter, to praise him set thy trumpets free !
He was a comrade and a friend to thee ;
Old age had ne'er a grander man than he —
     The snowy-haired Whittier !

VII.

O you who dwell in homes divinely fair,
With love and comfort smiling through the air,
With lives in mutual helpfulness so blessed,
That toil itself is harmony and rest,
He lives with you, and comforts you the while :
He makes your homes the brighter for his smile.

Your fireside borrows new and winsome glow
From the quaint Quaker hearth of long ago ;
To him the homage of your heart belongs ;
Your children are the sweeter for his songs.
He is a soul that will not be replaced ;
A guest whose absence cannot be effaced ;
    Your friend through smile or tear ;
And you whose life increasing wealth controls,
Till it would fain make prisoners of your souls,
Accept awhile from gilded jails release,
And walk with him in open fields of peace.
Find, strewn about, a wealth that hath not wings ;
Appraise the fortune hid in common things ;
Turn mortal dollars to immortal deeds,
Seek daily help with help for others' needs,
And learn from him, how mending hearts that break,
Will soothe the griefs you cannot shun, and make
    Your anguish less severe ;
This lesson con, of worth superlative :
He who upon our earth would truly live,
Must bend his efforts both to gain and give !
    So taught the great Whittier !

VIII.

You whose life-work misfortune strews with pain,
With agony of body, heart, or brain,
Turn from despair ; escape depression's net ;
You had a faithful friend — you have him yet !
His gallantry watched kindly on her way,
The humble maid that tossed the fragrant hay ;
His pity sought the fallen conquered brave,
And left its tears upon an Indian grave ;
With flowers of justice and of love he strewed
The witch's child, by zealotry pursued ;
Even the soul in endless darkness thrown,
Had pity from his muse ; there was no moan
    Escaped his eager ear !
He pitied, with brave words that echo yet,
Th' old soldier, prisoned for a paltry debt ;

He helped to give a new and honored place
To an unjustly subjugated race ;
And though of peaceful lineage and creed,
Yet he could fight, when conflict was the need ;
And he could mould the silver of his song
In solid shot, to hurl 'gainst shame and wrong ;
And tyrants fell, and fetters burst in twain,
Before the fierce artillery of his brain.

  He recked not blow or sneer ;
Though followed by the menace of the knave,
Though round his presence senseless mobs might rave,
Injustice never found a foe more brave,
  Than hero-souled Whittier !

IX.

Greet him in Heaven ! Make his reception grand,
O earth-born poets of the farther land !
You who, with blindness blotting every joy,
Sang, and still sing, the funeral dirge of Troy,
Meet one, who, earthly passions risen above,
Worshiped a God of justice and of love !
You who with epics decked the heights of Rome,
This western poet glorified his home ;
Drink from his placid spirit's gentle rills,
O sad-faced exile from fair Florence' hills ;
You who, bard of Eternity and Time,
Made even the loss of Paradise sublime,
  Greet him as friend and peer !
Thou, Prince of Stratford — England's flaming star,
Thou, laureate loved, who lately " crossed the bar ; "
Thou, Concord sage, by whose great heart and head,
Philosophy and poetry were wed :
Swan of the Charles, who, in progressive calm,
Gave to the world life's thrilling trumpet psalm ;
All you who are the brightest and the best,
With intellect as well as goodness blessed,
And all who humbly toiled from day to day,
With but the hope of Heaven to light your way,

Hail him as comrade dear!
And grant, O God, his spirit may extend
Through all this earth, till days and nights shall end ;
Our citizen, our poet, and our friend —
  The starry-crowned Whittier!

The quartette then sang

MY BIRTHDAY.

Beneath the moonlight and the snow
  Lies dead my latest year;
The winter winds are wailing low
  Its dirges in my ear.

I grieve not with the moaning wind
  As if a loss befell;
Before me, even as behind,
  God is, and all is well!

His light shines on me from above,
  His low voice speaks within, —
The patience of immortal love
  Outwearying mortal sin.

Not mindless of the growing years
  Of care and loss and pain,
My eyes are wet with thankful tears
  For blessings which remain.

If dim the gold of life has grown,
  I will not count it dross,
Nor turn from treasures still my own
  To sigh for lack and loss.

The years no charm from Nature take;
  As sweet her voices call,
As beautiful her mornings break,
  As fair her evenings fall.

.   .   .   .   .   .

Rest for the weary hands is good,
    And love for hearts that pine,
But let the manly habitude
    Of upright souls be mine.

Let winds that blow from heaven refresh,
    Dear Lord, the languid air;
And let the weakness of the flesh
    Thy strength of spirit share.

And, if the eye must fail of light,
    The ear forget to hear,
Make clearer still the spirit's sight,
    More fine the inward ear!

Be near me in mine hours of need
    To soothe, or cheer, or warn,
And down these slopes of sunset lead
    As up the hills of morn!

When Mayor Burnham arose to introduce the eulogist he said, —

I regret that I must read to you the following letter: —

25 Buckingham St., CAMBRIDGE, MASS.,
December 17, 1892.

DEAR SIR, — I am sorry to say that it will not be prudent for me, in view of the condition of my health, to fulfill my engagement to address the citizens of Haverhill, and pay a tribute of respect to my dear old friend, Mr. WHITTIER. I am glad to be able to say that Mr. EDWIN D. MEAD has kindly consented to take my place, and will address you.

Very respectfully yours,

T. W. HIGGINSON.

While we deeply regret the illness that keeps from us one who knew Mr. WHITTIER so long and so well, and whose presence alone would have carried us back to the very midst of the life of the great poet, yet we are indeed fortunate that we are honored in having in his stead a gentleman perfectly familiar and in full sympathy with the aims and life purposes of the great man, and well qualified to voice our tribute to his worth.

I present to you EDWIN D. MEAD, of Boston.

Mr. MEAD then proceeded in an eloquent manner to pay his tribute to Mr. WHITTIER in the following address.

THE EULOGY.

By EDWIN D. MEAD.

In all the complete editions of Whittier's poems, there stands next to the title-page an introductory poem, — a proem. This proem, dated 1847, should be read carefully by every student of Whittier, for it is the poet's own deliberate overture, and gives as true a cue to his general work and purpose as an overture of Wagner's to the opera it belongs to. Not so pronounced, nor in respect to some important features of his work and genius so truly self-revealing or self-judging, as other passages which we may note, it is more general than any other; and for this reason, as well as because the poet himself has set it so permanently at the front, let us listen to it as a fitting text for all I have to say, as we consider here, the more seriously as we stand by our saintly and heroic poet's new-made grave, what he has done for America, the use which he has made of American themes, and the nature of his services for American life and thought : —

I love the old melodious lays
Which softly melt the ages through,
The songs of Spenser's golden days,
Arcadian Sidney's silvery phrase,
Sprinkling our noon of time with freshest morning dew.

Yet vainly in my quiet hours
To breathe their marvellous notes I try ;
I feel them as the leaves and flowers
In silence feel the dewy showers,
And drink with glad, still lips the blessing of the sky.

The rigor of a frozen clime,
The harshness of an untaught ear,
The jarring words of one whose rhyme
Beat often Labor's hurried time,
Or Duty's rugged march through storm and strife, are here.

Of mystic beauty, dreamy grace,
No rounded art the lack supplies ;
Unskilled the subtle lines to trace,
Or softer shades of Nature's face,
I view her common forms with unanointed eyes.

Nor mine the seer-like power to show
The secrets of the heart and mind ;
To drop the plummet-line below
Our common world of joy and woe,
A more intense despair or brighter hope to find.

Yet here at least an earnest sense
Of human right and weal is shown ;
A hate of tyranny intense,
And hearty in its vehemence,
As if my brother's pain and sorrow were my own.

O Freedom ! if to me belong
Nor mighty Milton's gift divine,
Nor Marvell's wit and graceful song,
Still with a love as deep and strong
As theirs, I lay, like them, my best gifts on thy shrine.

This portrait of himself is painted in humility, yet the humility is of the very substance of the poet's mind, and the lines it draws give us a truer image than the bolder assertions we ourselves should find just and necessary could outline. Bolder assertions we ourselves should have to make in justice. We could not grant the absence of the "seer-like power" or the "rounded art" in Whittier, or that it was with unanointed eyes that the poet looks on nature. It was upon her common forms, indeed, that he did chiefly look, but it was upon these, too, that Wordsworth chiefly looked, and Emerson. It was no unanointed eyes that saw the pictures which chase each other in swift panorama through the lines of "The Barefoot Boy." There was the same unction here which opened the greater poet's eyes to the subtle beauties sung in "Wood Notes." But this is the difference between Whittier's poems of nature and Emerson's, — that Emerson loves nature more for its own sake, while with Whittier the human interest is always interfused. We cannot dissociate the birds and bees and squirrels, the flowers and trees and the laughing brook, from the barefoot boy himself, and we enter more into his fresh, irresponsible joy in them than into their own beauty. Take, too, the poem on Monadnock, the subject also, as it chances, of one of Emerson's own poems of nature. The interest we are made to feel in the very charming, natural, and pastoral picture falls quite behind our interest in the homely words of the farmer : —

" Yes, most folks think it has a pleasant look ;
I love it for my good old mother's sake,
Who lived and died here in the peace of God."

" We felt," says the poet, —

We felt that man was more than his abode,
The inward life than Nature's raiment more ;
And the warm sky, the sundown-tinted hill,
The forest and the lake, seemed dwarfed and dim
Before the saintly soul whose human will
Meekly in the Eternal footsteps trod,
Making her homely toil and household ways
An earthly echo of the song of praise
Swelling from angel lips and harps of seraphim.

This absorption of nature in the human, this
subjection of nature to the human, is constant
with Whittier. The little poem, " The Hill-Top,"
follows precisely the same course of thought as that
from which I have quoted. " Snow-Bound " almost
throughout illustrates the idea.

" No rounded art," — the poet tells us that there
is no rounded art in what he brings us. This, too,
we cannot grant. It is true that Whittier cannot
be called an artist in that full sense in which Longfellow was an artist. There are few works of his
in which the artist's motive, the love of beauty and
of structure for their own sake, is the primary
motive.

Confess, old friend,

says the Traveler to the Poet, in " The Tent on the
Beach," —

your austere school
Has left your fancy little chance ;
You square to reason's rigid rule
The flowing outlines of romance.

With conscience keen from exercise,
And chronic fear of compromise,
You check the free play of your rhymes, to clap
A moral underneath, and spring it like a trap.

It is quite true that most of Whittier's poems
have been written for distinct moral ends, and that
the moral motive quite outranks the poetic motive,
as we read. It is what the Germans call *tendenz*
poetry, — poetry with an ulterior purpose; and
although to the realm of *tendenz* poetry belong
many lyric and didactic works which have vindi-
cated their claim to eternity, and which the lover
of beauty would not willingly let die, it is mostly,
by its very nature, ephemeral and of subordinate
worth in the world of art, whatever be its virtue in
the world of acting men, and whatever nobility of
thought and character it voices. Yet were old
Tyrtæus and the Corn-Law Rhymer true poets;
and Whittier would be a true poet if "Snow-
Bound" and "The Tent on the Beach" had never
been written, but only the "Songs of Labor" and
the "Voices of Freedom."

We find no dramas here, like "John Endicott;"
no complex, imposing work of art like the "Christus," few works at all of considerable magnitude
and sustained imagination, like "Hiawatha" or
"Evangeline." In certain of its services, "The
Pennsylvania Pilgrim" may be compared with
"The Courtship of Miles Standish," but certainly
not for a moment as a poem. In point of art, the
greatest of Whittier's works are "Snow-Bound"

and " The Tent on the Beach." " Snow-Bound "
seems to me as beautiful and perfect a poem as
" The Deserted Village " or " The Cotter's Saturday Night." " The Tent on the Beach " shows,
most distinctly of all the poet's works, the hand of
the artist, — the structural instinct and the love of
effect.   Like " The Wayside Inn " — our greatest
poem of " The Canterbury Pilgrims " order — in its
form, it certainly has not that work's rich compass,
its broad basis of culture, its varied imagination, is
not at all a work of such scope or pretension; but
it is a work of remarkable power and beauty,
variety and skill, and quite sufficient of itself to
show that our poet has a " rounded art."   And not
only in these larger works does this rounded art
appear, but such poems as " The Chapel of the
Hermits," " The Last Walk in Autumn," " The
Preacher," " The Barefoot Boy," " Maud Muller,"
and many of the New England Ballads, are most
artistic and perfect in their form and finish.

There is the rounded art in Whittier, and there
is also the "seer-like power."   "Nor mine," he
says, —

> the seer-like power to show
> The secrets of the heart and mind.

He means by it that he is not philosopher nor
theologian, that he has no light to throw upon the
deeper mysteries and problems of religion and
the soul.   Seer like Emerson, philosophic poet like
Tennyson, Whittier certainly is not.   His genius

THE WHITTIER ELM

altogether was of an essentially narrower order
than Tennyson's. But there is no other poet of
our time, after Tennyson, for whom the problems of
human life and destiny have had, if we may so
speak, a more irresistible fascination.

"Is it well," asks one listener of the Poet in
"The Tent on the Beach," —

> Is it well to pry
> Into the secrets which belong
> Only to God ?

But the Poet vindicates the right, and pleads the
duty, of the deepest searching of the Eternal purposes; and to these religious inquiries he himself
continually recurs. Nor can it be denied that he
does it to good purpose, and that by such poems as
"My Soul and I" and "The Eternal Goodness" he
has contributed very signally to the cause of the
new and better faith in America. I suppose that
most readers of Whittier would say that they value
him, next after his service for freedom and a truer
patriotism and citizenship, precisely for the more
inspiring religious insights he has helped them to,
and the broader and nobler view of the divine
government and nature. In no other of our
poets do we find such traces of the conflict with the
old New England Calvinism as in the pages of
Whittier, and it is for his help in freeing them from
the thraldom of that nightmare that many owe
him most. Whittier was born into a time and
place in which the merciless old theology was

5

supreme; and the more he came to know it, the more his Quaker soul recoiled and fought it.

And wider yet in thought and deed,

he sings to his old-time friend, in " Memories,"

> Diverge our pathways, one in youth ;
> Thine the Genevan's sternest creed,
> While answers to my spirit's need
> The Derby dalesman's simple truth ;

and again, in "The Eternal Goodness," —

> I trace your lines of argument ;
> Your logic linked and strong
> I weigh as one who dreads dissent,
> And fears a doubt as wrong.

> But still my human hands are weak
> To hold your iron creeds ;
> Against the words ye bid me speak
> My heart within me pleads.

It is that same protest and pleading cry of the crushed and bruised and outraged New England heart which we hear in Mrs. Stowe's "Oldtown Folks," in Sylvester Judd's "Margaret," and in Mr. Hollister's "Kinley Hollow." Whittier is preëminently the poet of this theological tragedy, — a tragedy which it is as essential for the foreigner to understand, before he can do justice to Whittier, as it is for us to understand the effects of the cornlaws before we can appreciate Ebenezer Elliott. Aside from the devotion to it of many of the religious lyrics and the incidental reflection of it in many of the larger works, it is the distinct occasion

and theme of several such briefer poems as " The
Minister's Daughter," and especially of that most
valuable of all echoes of the " Great Revival," and
one of the most thoughtful and finished of all of
Whittier's poems, " The Preacher." The portraits
of Edwards and Whitefield here, and the outline of
their powerful work, are most striking and memo-
rable, and most of all because of the fine justice
done them, and the deep, sympathetic recognition
of the sincere and awful earnestness of the great
preachers, and of the genuinely prophetic in them.
Throughout all the terrible upheaval, the poet
tells us, while all others shook and burned with the
volcanic fires, —

> The Quaker kept the way of his own, —
> A non-conductor among the wires,
> With coat of asbestos proof to fires :
> And, quite unable to mend his pace
> To catch the falling manna of grace,
> He hugged the closer his little store
> Of faith, and silently prayed for more ;
> And, vague of creed and barren of rite,
> But holding, as in his Master's sight,
> Act and thought to the inner light,
> The round of his simple duties walked,
> And strove to live what the others talked.

It was the Quaker in Whittier, the reverence of
the inner light above all outward claim or revelation, which formed the point of contact between
him and Emerson and the Transcendentalists, and
which made him a regular, direct, and efficient
factor in the reform of religion in New England

of which Emerson was the leader.   For indeed, so
far as their first religious principle goes, Quakerism and Transcendentalism are one.   And if our
sweet and humble Quaker poet had not indeed the
"seer-like power" of the great Transcendentalist,
he was still a seer by very virtue of the religion
which he was faithful to, and has proved himself a
seer by the many gates ajar which he has left for
many.

Returning, therefore, to our proem, what do we
say ?   That Whittier does not get at Nature's
secrets with the penetrating power of Emerson or
of Wordsworth, that he has not the rounded art of
Longfellow, nor the philosophy of Tennyson or Emerson, but that he is, nevertheless, true seer, true
artist, and true interpreter of Nature.

Yet, in disclaiming these high titles and telling
us that, if indeed he has small right to these, his
work does show at least an earnest sense of human
right, a hate of tyranny, a hearty sympathy with
all men's pain and sorrow, and a love of freedom as
deep and strong as that of Marvell or of Milton, —
in putting these distinctly in the foreground, Whittier puts in the foreground what belongs there, and
what alone, perhaps, will give him any lasting or
long remembrance in America.   He will not live
as a poet of nature, and few of his works will be
given permanence by their mere artistic beauty.
His religious poems will, indeed, long maintain
their wholesome currency, — none of our poets has
written so much that we can make good hymns of ;

but when these, too, have become unfashionable
and forgotten, Whittier will still be heartily remembered for his songs of freedom and equality, for
the lessons of toleration which he has drawn from
the chapters of our early history, and especially
as the poet preëminently of the anti-slavery conflict. His highest credential as a poet is precisely
that which makes him a poet of America.

If it is as the simple and sometimes rude poet of
freedom and human brotherhood that Whittier has
the greatest claim upon us, this is not, as I have
already said, because he had not the capacity for
melodious lays which, if not indeed as marvelous
as the songs of Spenser or the silvery phrase of
Sidney, should still be rich in dreamy grace and
mystic beauty, but because, amid the visions of
beauty which blessed the poet's eye and the summer sounds which filled his ear, the spirit of the
man saw other sights and heard another sound, —

> A deeper sound that drowned them all,
> A voice of pleading choked with tears,
> The call of human hopes and fears,
> The Macedonian cry to Paul !

" Oh, not of choice," he sings as an epilogue to
" The Panorama," —

> Oh, not of choice, for themes of public wrong
> I leave the green and pleasant paths of song, —
> The mild, sweet words which soften and adorn,
> For griding taunt and bitter laugh of scorn.
> More dear to me some song of private worth.
> Some homely idyl of my native North,

Some summer pastoral of her inland vales
Or, grim and weird, her winter fireside tales
Haunted by ghosts of unreturning sails, —
Lost barks at parting hung from stem to helm
With prayers of love, like dreams on Virgil's elm.

And, if no song of idlesse I have sung,
Nor tints of beauty on the canvas flung, —
If the harsh numbers grate on tender ears,
And the rough picture overwrought appears, —
With deeper coloring, with a sterner blast,
Before my soul a voice and vision passed,
Such as might Milton's jarring trump require,
Or glooms of Dante fringed with lurid fire.

He turned from the purely poetic life to the
tumult of affairs for the same reason that Milton
himself did it, for the same reason that was ever
sweeping Fichte away from philosophic specula-
tion to the pulpit and the rostrum, and that made
Robertson of Brighton, with that fine sensibility
and critical insight by which he could have earned
so brilliant a place in the pure fields of literature,
preacher instead of essayist, — because the crying
wrongs and needs of humanity rang so loudly in
his ears that he could no other than speak directly
then and there for God and the right. Much more
self-confessing than Longfellow, Whittier's pages
abound with passages like that I have quoted,
freely sharing with us his moral and poetic mo-
tives. The little poems, " My Namesake," " My
Triumph," and " My Birthday," all get their value
from what of this is in them.

It is peculiarly fitting and grateful that the

preëminent poet of the anti-slavery struggle should
have been one who, like Elliott in England and the
great singer of " A man's a man for a' that," rose
up directly from the ranks of the common people,
and spoke with no prestige of wealth, high pedigree, or university, but with the simple power of
a universal truth of humanity. It is true that
there was no American poet who, when slavery
raised its dreadful head and threatened with its
poison the life of the state, was not found doing
valiant battle for freedom and the primal rights
which make men men. Ever indeed the poet, be
he scholar or peasant, is predestinated and divinely
called to the service of the true and good, and
cannot serve the wrong ; for if he seek to do it,
then does the poet in him wither and perish, the
God-intrusted genius is inevitably withdrawn, and
the inspiring fountain flows no more. Yet was the
preëminent poet of the anti-slavery struggle not
Longfellow nor Lowell nor Emerson nor Holmes,
but this man of the common people.

Not born like Longfellow into an atmosphere of
culture and the beckonings of easy opportunity, not
trained like him in college halls in the companionship of Æschylus, Theocritus, and Pindar, he was
not borne to the summit of Parnassus by the wings
of griffins, nor by any silvery chariot along the Attic
turnpike, but climbed the rugged mountain-side
alone, unaided save by shepherd's crook, from the
rude hamlets of the peasants at the base. He did
not exercise on the seven hills of Rome, nor see the

Italian sun go down among the Italian pines behind
St. Peter's dome.   He did not stand by Virgil's
grave upon the Neapolitan hill, nor by exiled
Dante's empty tomb in Santa Croce.   He did not
look upon the canvas of Raphael, nor the marble
of Michael Angelo.   He did not see Mont Blanc
against the sky, the creeping glacier, the rushing
avalanche. nor hear the music of the Staubbach
or Schaffhausen's roar.   He did not walk amid
the soft, green borders of blue Leman, Eden of the.
poets. nor by the darker waters consecrated by
the vows of the men of Rutli.   He did not see the
Danube from Walhalla, nor linger through long
summer days among the legend-haunted castles of
the Rhine.   He did not feel the awful hush of Wit-
tenberg and Weimar and Stratford ; he did not see
the red procession which sweeps through the Place
of Peace, nor the crimson tides of Palace Yard and
Tower Hill.   He did not hear Te Deums echoed
from the vaulted roofs of Gothic minsters ; he did
not see the sky which bends o'er England's abbeys,
nor dream among the ivied walls by the Isis and
Cam.   The roar of London, the majesty of West-
minster, the sanctity of Bemerton Church and Bed-
ford Jail. the double charm of Grasmere, sweet
Innisfallen. Ellen's Isle, the Brigs of Ayr, — all the
great inspirations which these things bring to him
who lives among them, the visions of beauty which
they open, above all, to the clairvoyant eye of the
poet, their tempering, suggesting, broadening, and
rounding offices, it was not his to benefit by.   His

Parthenon was the pine meeting-house, and his Academy the common school. His Ilissus has been the Merrimack, and his Tempe the valley of the Pemigewasset; his nectar the sweet cider of October, and his ambrosia the Thanksgiving pumpkin pie. Not his to gather of the rich fruits in the long-cultivated fields of history, romance, and song, but to pioneer in our green forests, and plant in the yet virgin soil of the New England clearings.

Whittier's longing interest, indeed, went out towards the sacred grounds of history, as his love went out to the songs of Spenser and the silvery phrase of Sidney; but that which was to Longfellow and Lowell subject of familiar experience was to him only the subject of dreams: —

> I know not how, in other lands,
>   The changing seasons come and go :
> What splendors fall on Syrian sands,
>   What purple lights on Alpine snow :
> Nor how the pomp of sunrise waits
> On Venice at her watery gates ;
> A dream alone to me is Arno's vale,
> And the Alhambra's halls are but a traveler's tale.

Yet, though his thoughts of other lands were dreams alone, he still has dreamed his dreams, and scattered through his pages many charmingly imagined foreign pictures.

It was chiefly to Palestine that his fond fancy traveled, the Holy Land of the Bible story: —

> Blest land of Judea ! thrice hallowed of song,
> Where the holiest of memories pilgrim-like throng,

> In the shade of thy palms, by the shores of thy sea,
> On the hills of thy beauty, my heart is with thee.

But the poet consoles himself, in the lack of the privilege to have walked in these sacred places, with the thought that far more beautiful and sacred than the rocks of Tabor or the waters of Galilee is the Spirit which transfigured them, and which, perennial and omnipresent, may transfer what is most precious in their transfiguration to our own hills and dales and hearths and homes, making

> Our common daily life divine,
> And every land a Palestine.

The moral interest is always supreme and immediate with Whittier, and, whatever his interest in the classic grounds of poetry and history, the inability to visit them could not possibly be to him the deprivation or the disadvantage that it would have been to Longfellow, with his subtle sense of association, and his eye so much more the slave of sensuous beauty.

He lived on in the narrow bounds of his native Essex, very content with his " fireside travels;" very thankful for such gifts as the gods sent; very sure that nine tenths of everything is in the thinking, and that good fancy is much more than great privilege; very hearty to make the most of Newburyport Lighthouse, since the Pharos would not answer his bell, and to catch the story of the Merrimack, since the Jordan was not behind the house.

His were not the stimulating intellectual sur-

roundings of the university town or the capital;
his daily companions not, like those of Longfellow
and Lowell, the scholars and poets of Boston and
Cambridge. but the simple farmers and craftsmen
of a New England village; and he was a shy and
rare visitor to the great towns and the literary so-
cieties. Yet was the solitude of Amesbury no
dull and vacant solitude.

> What lack of goodly company,
>   When masters of the ancient lyre
> Obey my call, and trace for me
>   Their words of mingled tears and fire!
> I talk with Bacon, grave and wise:
> I read the world with Pascal's eyes:
> And priest and sage. with solemn brows austere,
> And poets. garland-bound, the lords of thought draw near.

It is a great mistake to look upon Whittier as a
rude, unlettered poet, simply breathing through a
rustic reed the notes of a nobly human but yet un-
disciplined thought. There are few men, indeed,
who give much to the world save by taking much
from the world. The great creators are also the
faithful lovers and users of great precedent crea-
tions. Burns does not draw his inspirations simply
from the mountain daisies of Mauchline, the rip-
plings of the Ayr, the bright eyes of Highland las-
sies, and his own fresh heart's hot beatings, but
also from Pope's translation of Homer, from Rich-
ardson's " Pamela," from odd volumes of the " Spec-
tator," from the " History of the Bible," and from
Derham and Ray on the " Wisdom and Power of

God." To mornings at the plough there followed evenings with Euclid, the French grammar, and " Telemachus." Burns was a good French scholar. To say that he was a Scotchman is almost to say that he knew his Bible and his catechism well, and his verses everywhere say how much more than the mere Scotchman's training he had in this great university of a poet. He reveled in the old Border Ballads, he hungrily devoured the works of the great Scotch and English poets, and Virgil was his own familiar friend. Yet cannot we properly call Burns a *scholar.* With much greater justice may we give that name to Whittier. If lacking, indeed, the Harvard *imprimatur,* he did not fail to find, in his own way, the world's good books ; and Emerson has wisely said that the best which the university does for a man is to put him in intelligent possession of the keys to the library. Not Bacon and Pascal only has Whittier had to his friends, not only Spenser and Sidney and Milton and Marvell, but a very great and goodly fellowship of the poets, priests, and sages of all lands and ages. His " Songs of Three Centuries " — surely one of the best of the anthologies — is alone sufficient to show the largeness of his knowledge of our modern literature, and the discipline and excellence of his literary judgment. If he did not easily command the tongues of Homer and of Virgil, he was at home in the language and the thought of Tauler and Eckhart, and he translates the songs of Lamartine. The Bible has been as very a part of his

regular sustenance as his daily bread ; and he loved
the great doctors of the church, Ambrose, Anselm,
— quotes fondly Augustine's " Soliloquies." He
paraphrases maxims from the " Mahabarata " and
the " Institutes " of Manu, prefixes to his " Snow-
Bound," along with the familiar lines from Emerson, a text from the " Occult Philosophy " of Cor-
nelius Agrippa, and fortifies his use of the customs
of the Kolfolk by appeal to the " Journal of the
Asiatic Society." He delved into the old Norse
legends, into the habits of the Hindoos, and into a
great literature of voyages and travels. He worked
in the rich mines of sacred and legendary art, and
wrote feeling and discriminating lines upon Raphael and Tintoretto. How much of careful
thought and of broad and genuine culture, can-
celling all small and vulgar prejudice, is revealed
in that one profound and beautiful poem of " The
Chapel of the Hermits," with its tenderly just
picture of Rousseau ! How truly erudite a work,
in its limited sphere, is " The Pennsylvania Pilgrim "! Every chapter of the history and literature of Quakerism — Fox, Barclay, Penn, John
Woolman — was as familiar to Whittier as the
tales of childhood. Equally familiar all that per-
tains to the history of slavery and the struggle for
freedom the wide world over. It is not only with
the New England reformers that he works, but
with an interest equally direct, intelligent, and out-
spoken he pleads the cause and celebrates the
successes or laments the checks of the reformers of

England and of Italy, of Poland, Hungary, and
Brazil. To North and South and East and West,
the windows of his busy study opened, and each
morn has brought to each his returning carrier
doves, with their tidings of foreboding or the olive-
branch of hope.

But chiefly to the history and life of America,
and in particular his own New England, have the
poet's studies always been directed. The old
Indian legends, the stories of the French adven-
turers and of the Jesuit missionaries, the colonial
traditions, the Provincial records, the books of Mor-
ton, Mayhew, Winslow, Mather, and Roger Wil-
liams, the political and theological pamphlets, —
there has been no man more familiar with them,
no one to whom they have imparted more ; while
the course of our general politics, and especially
all that concerned the conflict with slavery, — the
proceedings of conventions, the debates of the Senate, whatever expressed the popular will, — could
not have been more minutely followed by the professional politician. Surely to him of whom we
say all this we cannot deny the name of scholar.

It is certainly interesting and notable, and to
the believer in the law of progress should be very
grateful, that the poet of New England *par excellence* should have risen from precisely that religious
sect which was the object of the most bitter persecution of the Puritan Fathers of New England.
It is a long way from the doings pictured in
Longfellow's " John Endicott " to the canonization

of Whittier in the Old South Meeting-house. The
iron has been tempered in many fires in two hundred years; though fidelity compels me to say
here that all those early Quakers were not like
Edith Christison, and that my own pretty firm
conviction is, that very many things are done in
this world in the name of religion for which it is
quite in order to whistle for the constable. By
which, of course, I do not mean to say that I do
not consider the Endicott and Mather régime
severe, unjustifiable, and wicked. Such it was, —
a period for which the most loyal and loving son
of New England must humbly ask for the broad
mantle of charity, a period to which we turn
simply for its lessons of warning. Whittier has
drawn from it many of these lessons; but he
writes of the persecution of the Quakers with no
more feeling of personal or sectarian grievance
than does Longfellow in "John Endicott," or
than he himself writes of that other New England tragedy, — the witchcraft horror. Whittier
was a very faithful Quaker, — very faithful to the
Quaker spirit and very tender of the Quaker traditions, though well emancipated from whatever
of superstition yet attaches to the Quaker Church,
the same kind of Quaker that Emerson was Puritan: Quaker in the essential reverence of the inner light, Puritan purified from the Puritan theology.

> In calm and cool and silence, once again
> I find my old accustomed place among

My brethren, where, perchance, no human tongue
Shall utter words ; where never hymn is sung,
Nor deep-toned organ blown, nor censer swung,
Nor dim light falling through the pictured pane.
There, syllabled by silence, let me hear
The still, small voice which reached the prophet's ear :
Read in my heart a still diviner law
Than Israel's leader on his tables saw.

To him there is a much higher than "It is written," and there are *many* names whereby men
may be saved, — whereby, indeed, they are and
have been saved. He holds

> That to be saved is only this, —
> Salvation from our selfishness,

and that in the work of this salvation mankind
has been appealed to by a great hierarchy of
prophets and mediators of the Eternal Goodness ;
while ever coöperant with this external revelation
and incitement is that spark of God within the
soul, the Inner Light, which lighteth every man
that cometh into the world. No smaller definition
of the Inner Light will satisfy this Quaker. He
thanks God

> for the faith which embraces the whole,
> Of the creeds of the ages the life and the soul,
> Wherein letter and spirit the same channel run,
> And man has not severed what God has made one, —
>
> For a sense of the Goodness revealed everywhere,
> As sunshine impartial, and free as the air ;
> For a trust in humanity, heathen or Jew,
> And a hope for all darkness the Light shineth through.

The Word which the reason of Plato discerned ;
The truth, as whose symbol the Mithra-fire burned ;
The soul of the world which the Stoic but guessed, —
In the Light Universal the Quaker confessed.

The most important by far of Whittier's Quaker poems is " The Pennsylvania Pilgrim." I have said that " The Pennsylvania Pilgrim " may be compared, in certain of its services, with " The Courtship of Miles Standish." As " The Court- ship of Miles Standish " brings before us more vividly and feelingly than any other work in our literature the life and spirit of Puritan Plymouth, in like manner does " The Pennsylvania Pilgrim " reproduce for us the spirit of the followers of Penn.

" The Pilgrims of Plymouth," says Whittier in his valuable introduction to this poem, " have not lacked historian and poet. Justice has been done to their faith, courage, and self-sacrifice, and to the mighty influence of their endeavors to estab- lish righteousness on the earth. The Quakers of Pennsylvania, seeking the same object by different means, have not been equally fortunate."

The purpose of " The Pennsylvania Pilgrim " is to do poetic justice to the Quakers of Philadelphia, and especially to Daniel Pastorius and the little band of German Mystics, disciples of Spener, who founded the settlement of Germantown. Pastorius is the Pennsylvania Pilgrim, the combined Bradford and Brewster of the little colony ; and the noble character of Pastorius as Whittier paints it, and

6

the beautiful life led there upon the Schuylkill by
those simple German Pietists, are so charming that
our gratitude to the poet is mingled with a regret
almost as great, that history has so sadly neglected
this rare chapter in our American morning, — a
chapter interesting to the student of thought for
nothing more than for its showing of the mingling
with the Quaker element, upon our fresh American soil, of that stream of German Pietism in
which, in the Fatherland, Immanuel Kant was
reared, and to the permanent influence of which
the deeply religious tone of his philosophy is
largely due. A glance is given us here into another significant moment in the community of
Quakerism and Transcendentalism in pedigree and
quality.

This Pennsylvania colony was nobly faithful to
the principle of toleration and religious equality ;
and Whittier notes with special pleasure the fact
that, in the year 1688, Pastorius drew up a memorial against slave-holding, which was adopted by
the Germantown Friends and sent up to the Yearly
Meeting at Philadelphia. This was the first protest made by a religious body against negro
slavery.

The poet is very merciful toward the Massachusetts Puritans, when he has to bring them into
contrast with these Pennsylvania Quakers, his
kindness even prompting him to charge something
of the intolerant temper of the Puritans to the
Boston east winds, whose fretting and demoralizing

influence they had to bear. The Philadelphia
skies were tender and the air caressing. But
" who knows," the poet asks,

> what goadings in their sterner way
> O'er jagged ice, relieved by granite gray,
> Blew round the men of Massachusetts Bay ? —
>
> What hate of heresy the east wind woke ?
> What hints of pitiless power and terror spoke
> In waves that on their iron coast-line broke ?

This bit of Buckle from the poet is certainly very
grateful to the man who has to take his January
walks on Boston Common, and hates to charge the
full sum of his ill-will towards those who interrupt
his course to his own innate depravity. But
though the east wind is certainly very provoking,
and doubtless wicked in its way, we fear that it
cannot be held altogether responsible for the New
England tragedies, whose moral Longfellow pointed
in " Giles Corey " and " John Endicott," and which
are reflected in Whittier's " Cassandra Southwick,"
" The King's Missive," and " The Witch's Daughter." We do not know that Salem is more windy
than Plymouth, and we do know that Roger Wil-
liams, whose praises Whittier himself has sung so
heartily, could think out his " Soul Liberty " in
Salem itself. No east wind could wither his great
soul. And what concerns our own day, — though
Whittier has had occasion to reproach some of our
own generation of priests for an intolerance, big-
otry, and hardness more miserable than any intoler-

ance of the Puritans, because born of no consuming
religious zeal like theirs, and without any of the
excuses of an age to which Spinoza and Taylor and
Lessing had not yet spoken, — I do not know that
these reproaches have been more provoked by the
bigots of windy Massachusetts than by those of
sunny Pennsylvania.

" The King's Missive " is the latest and perhaps
the most important of these poems of the era of
persecution.   Its subject is the historical incident,
also introduced into Longfellow's " John Endicott,"
with which the persecution of the Quakers ceased,
— the bringing of the command from King Charles
to set the sufferers free.   It is a very dramatic
scene between the old governor and Samuel Shat-
tuck, the Quaker bearer of the missive ; and it is a
very touching scene when the doors of the jail are
opened and the young and the old — one who had
been appointed to die — came forth with thanksgiving into the lanes and alleys of the town, amid
the mingled scoffing and pity : —

> One brave voice rose above the din.
> Upsall, gray with his length of days,
> Cried from the door of his Red Lion Inn :
> " Men of Boston, give God the praise !
> No more shall innocent blood call down
> The bolts of wrath on your guilty town.
> The freedom of worship, dear to you,
> Is dear to all, and to all is due.
>
> " I see the vision of days to come,
> When your beautiful City of the Bay
> Shall be Christian liberty's chosen home,
> And none shall his neighbor's rights gainsay :

> The varying notes of worship shall blend,
> And as one great prayer to God ascend,
> And hands of mutual charity raise
> Walls of salvation and gates of praise."

And so, concludes the poet, —

> passed the Quakers through Boston town,
> Whose painful ministers sighed to see
> The walls of their sheep-fold falling down,
> And wolves of heresy prowling free.
> But the years went on, and brought no wrong ;
> With milder counsels the state grew strong,
> As outward Letter and inward Light
> Kept the balance of truth aright.

> The Puritan spirit, perishing not,
> To Concord's yeomen the signal sent,
> And spake in the voice of the cannon-shot
> That severed the chains of a continent.
> With its gentler mission of peace and good-will
> The thought of the Quaker is living still,
> And the freedom of soul he prophesied
> Is gospel and law where the martyrs died.

Thus the black cloud rolled away, and the day when it darkened the New England sky seems happily farther away than the day when Boston was yet the Indian's verdant Shawmut, discordant Salem peaceful Naumkeag, and the echoes of the white man's axe in the forests by the Merrimack had not yet disturbed the Sagamores of Agawam.

It is refreshing indeed to turn, with the poet, from the inhumanities of Salem witchcraft to the sylvan scenes of "The Bridal of Penacook," sad even as that beautiful Indian poem is. I can here hardly touch upon the Indian poems. "Mogg

Megone," the long poem printed first in the volumes of Whittier's Poems, but of which Whittier himself afterwards spoke disparagingly, is interesting only for its picture of the devotion of the Jesuit missionaries. A very beautiful little poem is "The Fountain," which preserves the tradition of a strange Indian coming back and looking down from a hill-top upon the old scenes, transformed by the new civilization, and then turning sadly away: —

> Naked lay, in sunshine glowing,
>   Hills that once had stood,
> Down their sides the shadows throwing
>   Of a mighty wood.
> Where the deer his covert kept,
> And the eagle's pinion swept!
>
> Where the birch canoe had glided
>   Down the swift Powow,
> Dark and gloomy bridges strided
>   Those clear waters now ;
> And where once the beaver swam
> Jarred the wheel and frowned the dam.
>
> For the wood-bird's merry singing
>   And the hunter's cheer,
> Iron clang and hammer's ringing
>   Smote upon his ear ;
> And the thick and sullen smoke
> From the blackened forges broke.
>
> Could it be his fathers ever
>   Loved to linger here ?
> These bare hills, this conquered river, —
>   Could they hold them dear.
> With their native loveliness
> Tamed and tortured into this ?

A pleasing parallel and contrast to this Indian picture is " Cobbler Keezar's Vision." Cobbler Keezar was a noted character among the first settlers in the valley of the Merrimack; and the poet makes the old German use his lapstone as a lens through which he looks a hundred and fifty years down the future. He too, like the Indian, sees the mighty forest broken and the broad land full of farms and mill-wheels, of villages and steeples; but the vision makes him glad and merry, and not sad. It was the vision of that New England into which the poet himself was born, and which he has loved so well. It is with New England eyes that Whittier has looked out on the world, and everything that he has written seems to have the New England country in the background and to be bathed in the New England air. So strong and diffusive is this local coloring, that it is doubtful, after all, whether many will ever love or properly appreciate the Essex poet save with a general knowledge of the New England life and history. I have said that " Snow-Bound " is to me a poem as dear and beautiful as " The Deserted Village " or " The Cotter's Saturday Night; " yet, as I make the comparison a second time, I think I see that " Snow-Bound " lacks something of the universality of these, and could not be as dear and beautiful as they to him who was not reared in a New England home. Its occasional lines of quite Wordsworthian doggerel could be forgiven; but, while Burns's peasant and Sweet Auburn are easily transfigured into what is common to every experience, only in America have there been such households as this one, snow-bound thus.

Essentially American, too, is " The Barefoot Boy." No defiant scion, he, of the rag-tag and bob-tailed class of a stratified society, but a genuine Yankee barefoot boy whose torn brim is an honest crown, whose veins are full of eagle's blood and who is heir-apparent to nothing less than the White House. And the " Songs of Labor " are all songs of New England labor, — the ship-builders and shoe-makers and drovers and fishermen and huskers and lumbermen, all men who were born within sound of the Merrimack.

To the American, Whittier has made the Merrimack and the Essex country almost as classic as Burns has made the banks and braes of Ayr and Doon. The very Tiber and the Rhine have had no more faithful celebrant, at least, than the Merrimack in Whittier. Its waters roar or murmur through many of the shorter poems. We follow it, with the poet, to its springs among the New Hampshire hills; and we learn to love the legends and the very church-spires of the villages that cluster upon its banks as it nears the ocean. " The Tent on the Beach " is pitched so near to where its waters mingle with the Atlantic that as the evening silence falls on the three friends, they hear the tolling of the bells in Newbury's steeples. Perhaps the greater part of Whittier's prose works, so far as they are not concerned with anti-slavery

THE BROOK

"The music of whose liquid lip
Had been to us companionship,
And, in our lonely life, had grown
To have an almost human tone."

and other humanitarian movements of the day, have to do with the Essex history, legends and life; and his one story is an Essex story, and not, like " Hyperion," a story of Heidelberg, Interlaken and the Rhine.

But dearer far to Whittier than the New England hills and villages, dearer than Essex and the Merrimack, has been the New England spirit and idea. He has been faithful and fond New Englander chiefly because New England has stood so faithfully for that freedom of the soul and that moral force for which he himself has stood, still kept her keen air native for a sense of duty as stalwart as Abraham Davenport's, and for an aspiration for perfection as innate and masterful as John Underhill's.

The riches of the commonwealth
Are free, strong minds, and hearts of health;
And more to her than gold or grain,
The cunning hand and cultured brain.

For well she keeps her ancient stock,
The stubborn strength of Pilgrim Rock;
And still maintains, with milder laws
And clearer light, the Good Old Cause!

Nor heeds the sceptic's puny hands,
While near her school the church-spire stands;
Nor fears the blinded bigot's rule,
While near her church-spire stands the school.

This was the Massachusetts which, when the accursed upas-tree of slavery was throwing out its roots in every direction with a terrible swiftness,

darkening the whole heaven with its branches and
poisoning all the air, infecting legislature and literature, school and church, until it seemed indeed
that the new democratic Canaan, heralded so highly
to waiting, praying Europe, was to become the by-
word of the nations and the " land of broken promise " — it was Massachusetts which then gave to
Freedom a tribune, a platform, a pulpit, and a newspaper — Garrison, Parker, Phillips, and Sumner.
It was natural and fitting that Massachusetts should
give a poet too, — and she did.

Whittier has said that, though he is not careless
of literary fame, he values more than any honor
for anything which he has written the honor of
having been of those who signed the call to the
first anti-slavery convention. He became at once
the secretary of the American Anti-Slavery Society and the editor successively of two anti-slavery
newspapers. Many of his essays, also, — as the
stinging review of Carlyle and " The Two Proces-
sions," — were written in the immediate service of
the reform. But his essays and editorials did very
little beside his inspired, indignant verses, which
rang through the idolatrous and sinful nation as
from the trump upon the mount of God.

There is scarcely any phase of the wrong and
horror of the slave's condition which he failed to
picture and almost no moment of the fight for
freedom which is not reflected in his lines. Such
pictures as those in " The Slave Ship," " The Hunters of Men," " The Farewell of the Virginia

Slave Mother," and "A Christian up for Sale," could never be forgotten by any into whom their lines had once been burned. When such scenes as these were daily, and lawful under the sun, through half the nation, while the "cant of Democracy dwelt on the lips of the forgers of fetters and wielders of whips," the very stones had cried out if men had been silent. Well might the impassioned poet cry:

Is this the land our fathers loved,
The freedom which they toiled to win?
Is this the soil whereon they moved?
Are these the graves they slumber in?
Are *we* the sons by whom are borne
The mantles which the dead have worn?

Shall tongues be mute, when deeds are wrought
Which well might shame extremest hell?
Shall freemen lock the indignant thought?
Shall pity's bosom cease to swell?
Shall Honor bleed? shall Truth succumb?
Shall pen and press and soul be dumb?

No; by each spot of haunted ground,
Where Freedom weeps her children's fall, —
By Plymouth's rock, and Bunker's mound, —
By Griswold's stained and shattered wall, —
By Warren's ghost, — by Langdon's shade, —
By all the memories of our dead!

By their enlarging souls, which burst
The bands and fetters round them set, —
By the free Pilgrim spirit nursed
Within our inmost bosoms, yet, —
By all above, around, below,
Be ours the indignant answer, — No!

Full of fire as these lines, taken almost at random from hundreds like them, are when read at any time, no one I suppose can appreciate their full heat and power who is not able in some way to reproduce the conditions and spirit of the time in which they appeared. Again and again the poet launched upon the winds that blew toward Carolina and Virginia the voice of the spirit of Plymouth Rock and Bunker Hill. Yet was he doomed to see New England herself drink the dregs of the cup of the nation's disgrace and fugitive slaves in chains marched down State Street, hedged by Massachusetts bayonets, over the very ground where the first blood of Freedom flowed in the war for independence, and in sight of Faneuil Hall itself, to be rendered back to bondage.

The church Americanized its prayer-book by the omission of the black man from Ary Scheffer's " Christus Consolator," which it had engraved for a fiontispiece ; the Nehemiah Adamses preached their " South-side " gospels in the Boston pulpits; and the various orthodoxies promulgated their " Pastoral Letters," begging the faithful to frown down the Garrisonian fuss and not be distracted by it from the serene service of the Lord. It is scarcely satirical to say, as Whittier represents in his cutting poem, that fugitive slaves were rendered up to the hunters on the Sabbath day in the church itself, whither they had flown for refuge, the parson himself leaving his pulpit to lend a hand.

It is a melancholy and humiliating chapter in which is written the history of the American Church in those anti-slavery days — never, save in exceptional instances, reaching a warm hand to the reformers, barely noticing them at all save by way of derogation or anathema, coming bodily to the moral side at last only when the battle had been fought and the popular tide was fully turned. The church had eaten the cotton hasheesh as well as the statesman, the judge, and the democrat, and Law and Gospel were dancing dervish dances in its distorted vision.

The whole great North presented to the poet in those early days of the reform the spectacle of a drugged people devoting " six days to Mammon, one to Cant, " —

> Official piety, locking fast the door
> Of Hope against three million souls of men, —
> Brothers, God's children, Christ's redeemed, — and then,
> With uprolled eyeballs and on bended knee
> Whining a prayer for help to hide the key !

What he saw in the Church, that also he saw in the Senate — one long succession of sops thrown to the monster, until at last Webster himself, the hope and strength of New England, went over to the ranks of the compromisers. Only in Theodore Parker's great address do we find the bitter disappointment and feeling of irreparable loss and pain which this act caused the anti-slavery men so deeply expressed as in the lines which Whittier wrote — the poem " Ichabod."

So fallen! so lost! the light withdrawn
    Which once he wore !
The glory from his gray hairs gone
    Forevermore !

.   .   .   .

Of all we loved and honored, naught
    Save power remains, —
A fallen angel's pride of thought,
    Still strong in chains.

All else is gone ; from those great eyes,
    The soul has fled :
When faith is lost, when honor dies,
    The man is dead!

In these last years, when passions have begun
to subside, Whittier has written of Webster again,
as if to atone for what might have been too one-
sided and severe in the earlier poem and do the
fullest justice to Webster's true nobility and great-
ness. It is, perhaps, no longer fair for any of
us to read " Ichabod " without also reading " The
Lost Occasion." Some men die too late, the poet
says, and some too soon. Webster died too soon.
Had he lived a decade longer, to see the full
venom and implacableness of the slave power, —
lived to see the star-flag of the Union fall from
Sumter and armed rebellion move on Washington,
then we cannot doubt how he had manifested his
nobler self and what a leader he had been in the
strife.

But it was almost impossible that the smitten
and grieved reformers should so forecast the years
in 1850, do even justice then to the great states-

man, or think of much besides the bitter blow of
his terrible mistake. And yet I am deeply and
chiefly impressed in reading such an address as
Parker's, prepared in the very furnace of the disappointment, by its judicialness and careful equity,
the manifest anxiety to recognize Webster's real
loftiness, and the satisfaction of all fair demands of
the historian to-day.

That 7th of March, 1850, marks perhaps the
lowest point of our national degradation. There
was no lower depth that we could touch, no sop
that we could throw the monster more precious
than the great defender of our Constitution and
our greatest man; and from that hour all that was
heroic in the land, shuddering at the fate forecast
by politicians' compromises, nerved itself for the
conflict which was irrepressible, and men's consciences smote miserable and wicked makeshifts
until, in ten years, Abraham Lincoln was placed at
the nation's forefront, armed with the nation's
sword.

Whittier, by very virtue of his Quakerism, is
opposed to war and physical force. He could engage in no warfare but a moral one, with the
weapons of Light and Truth and Love. He could
recognize the generous purpose of John Brown,
but he shrank back in horror from Harper's Ferry.
When it was evident, at last, that only the sword
could save the Union, he even said, Let the South
go, —

> Let us press
> The golden cluster on our brave old flag
> In closer union, and, if numbering less,
> Brighter shall shine the stars which still remain.

Yet he soon came to see clearly the short-sight-edness of such a policy, and to wait patiently while the terrible penalty of sin was paid.

> Not as we hoped, in calm of prayer,
>   The message of deliverance comes,
>   But heralded by roll of drums
> On waves of battle — troubled air! —
>
> Not as we hoped — but what are we?
>   Above our broken dreams and plans
>   God lays, with wiser hand than man's,
> The corner-stones of liberty."

Whittier was a most absolute and religious democrat. His greatest pride as an American was that America is the great bearer of the democratic idea. The prime significance to him of our great struggle was, perhaps, its significance to the nations of the old world, looking to us to prove that the republic can be trusted, as they painfully struggle towards it. His very soul reddened within him as he contemplated our infidelities and felt the irony of our sermons and our sympathy for Mazzini and Kossuth, while every fold of our own flag was stained and it was scorned on every shore as the symbol of a canting fiction and a hollow mockery. Yet did he never doubt the glorious issue, and never check the outflow of his generous and confident sympathies with the reformers of

France and Italy and England, while he worked
steadily on for his own land's redemption.   Never
did he shrink, even when clouds were thickest,
from identifying Europe's cause with ours nor
from declaring that the death to privilege which
should surely come in the New World meant also
death to privilege in the Old.

> Hear it, old Europe! we have sworn
>   The death of slavery. — When it falls,
> Look to your vassals in their turn,
> Your poor dumb millions, crushed and worn,
>   Your prisons and your palace walls !
>
> O kingly mockers ! — scoffing show
>   What deeds in Freedom's name we do ;
> Yet know that every taunt ye throw
> Across the waters, goads our slow
>   Progression towards the right and true.
>
> Not always shall your outraged poor,
>   Appalled by democratic crime,
> Grind as their fathers ground before ;
> The hour which sees our prison door
>   Swing wide shall be *their* triumph time !
>
> On then, my brothers ! every blow
>   Ye deal is felt the wide earth through.
> Whatever here uplifts the low,
> Or humbles Freedom's fateful foe,
>   Blesses the Old World through the New.

And so it is, my friends.   To us has been com-
mitted the leadership of the nations in the march
to freedom and the equal rights of men.   Such

7

is our birthright and great duty. We may not, in any false humility, disclaim the honor. Let us not, in the besetting temptations to luxury and levity which our great plenty breeds, come short in the sacred office. Let us know well that slavery is no mere thing of negroes and plantations, but a protean hydra, scotched but never killed, with which we have to war till doomsday. If conquered in one form then be we sure that it is gathering its strength to attack us in another; and let us give less care to celebration of our victories than to determining well the yet vulnerable points in our society and in our souls. What great new oppression threatens to-day the people's rights? What doctrine are you cherishing that makes the narrow mind? Our duty as Americans is not discharged so long as any crushing inequality of privilege remains and men are born and live without a chance, or until our society and institutions are so ordered as to give facility to every man and woman to grow up unto the fullness of the measure of Christian liberty. This is the American idea. This it is, or nothing, for which America stands among the nations and in history — the fullness of freedom, equality of privilege, and mutual obligation. Freedom and brotherhood — this is the saintly poet's burden, this the meaning to him of Plymouth and Concord and Gettysburg, this the song of our murmuring rivers, this the whisper of our pine-trees, this the commandment thundered by Niagara, this the pure gospel of our snowy mountains, this the bright promise of our sunset skies. Let us in reverence hear the poet's word, and let his finger touch our eye and heart, that we may see the beauties and the duties which he saw, and know that the place whereon we stand is holy ground.

These home-seen splendors are the same
Which over Eden's sunsets came ;
This mapled ridge shall Horeb be,
You green-banked lake our Galilee !

To these bowed heavens let wood and hill
Lift voiceless praise and anthem still ;
Fall, warm with blessing, over them,
Light of the New Jerusalem !

Henceforth my heart shall sigh no more
For olden time and holier shore ;
God's love and blessing, then and there,
Are now and here and everywhere.

Although there was a feeling of disappointment that Colonel HIGGINSON was debarred through illness from appearing, yet the enthusiasm with which Mr. MEAD was received, as well as the animated countenances of the cultured and critical audience and the close attention paid, bore testimony to the character of his eloquent and scholarly tribute.

CONCLUDING EXERCISES.

After the Oration the Mayor said : —

Before the " Auld Lang Syne" shall be sung that will close these exercises, let us pause that we may ask a question : —

Who does not remember the trying days when slavery had fastened its fangs upon this free country, and the instrumentalities that contributed to the overthrow of the monster evil? Foremost in this work with voice and pen was WHITTIER! But let us not forget his co-laborers and personal friends, some of whom lend their presence here to-day, and when we welcome the venerable JOHN W. HUTCHINSON, the last survivor of that matchless family whose patriotic songs did so much to hasten the glorious cause, we welcome them one and all. And for them he will briefly respond in song.

When Mr. HUTCHINSON arose to respond, the scene was touching in the extreme. A man he was on whom the hand of time had been laid, leaving its imprint in the snow-white locks that hung about his shoulders and the patriarchal beard that lay upon his breast. More than threescore and ten years had passed over his head ; sisters and brothers, old friends and associates, all had sung their last songs, and he, old and alone, stood there. His heavy brows still held their dark, strong shade, as if to add lustre to the keen, sharp eyes that, brightened by the occasion, flashed with the old-time fire ; his voice, weak with age, yet clear and sweet, fell upon his hearers as an echo from another age, a legacy handed down from a crisis when right was struggling close-matched against wrong.

He had come here to tune once more his lyre in honor of the dear friend of his youth and manhood.

After a few feeling remarks, in clear and melodious tones, he sang with wonderful effect, —

" EIN FESTE BURG IST UNSER GOTT."

(LUTHER'S HYMN.)

We wait beneath the furnace blast
The pangs of transformation :
Not painlessly doth God recast
And mould anew the nation.
Hot burns the fire
Where wrongs expire ;
Nor spares the hand
That from the land
Uproots the ancient evil.

What gives the wheat-field blades of steel ?
What points the rebel cannon?
What sets the roaring rabble's heel
On the old star-spangled pennon ?
What breaks the oath
Of the men o' the South ?
What whets the knife
For the Union's life ?
Hark to the answer — Slavery !

Then waste no blows on lesser foes
In strife unworthy freemen —
God lifts to-day the veil, and shows
The features of the demon !
O North and South,
Its victims both,

> Can ye not cry
> " Let slavery die ! "
> And union find in freedom ?

The exercises closed with " Auld Lang Syne," quartette and audience joining.

> Should auld acquaintance be forgot
>   And never brought to mind ?
> Should auld acquaintance be forgot
>   And days of auld lang syne ?
>
> For auld lang syne we meet to-day,
>   For auld lang syne
> We sing the songs our fathers sang,
>   In days of auld lang syne.
>
> Here we have met, here we may part
>   To meet on earth no more,
> And we may never meet again
>   The cherished friends of yore.
>
> For auld lang syne we meet to-day,
>   For auld lang syne
> We sing the songs our fathers sang,
>   In days of auld lang syne.

MR. WHITTIER AND HAVERHILL.

MR. WHITTIER AND HAVERHILL.

The interest for all that pertained to his native city was ever deep and strong in Mr. WHITTIER, and many were the exceedingly pleasant interchanges of mutual regard that passed between her citizens, her representatives, and himself.

This spirit he carried to the end, and that it was fully reciprocated is shown in the last correspondence that passed between him and the City Council, it being the occasion of his last BIRTHDAY.

IN BOARD OF ALDERMEN, *December* 17, 1891.

His Honor Mayor Burnham presiding.

On motion of the President of the Board, Alderman FRANK E. WATSON, the following was adopted : —

" On the anniversary of the birthday of our illustrious and honored friend, JOHN GREENLEAF WHITTIER, Esq., it is eminently fitting and appropriate that the City Government of Haverhill, the place of his birth and the home of his early years, should in some manner indicate their appreciation of his genius, their admiration of his pure and spotless life, and their gratitude for the services he has rendered to his country and to humanity.

We lay upon the altar of his fame the modest tribute of our esteem and love.

Passed unanimously by a rising vote.

Attest:

DAVID B. TENNEY,
City Clerk.

To this came the following touching reply : —

NEWBURYPORT, MASS., *Jan.* 4, 1892.

TO HIS HONOR THE MAYOR AND THE BOARD OF AL-
DERMEN OF THE CITY OF HAVERHILL.

GENTLEMEN, — I feel myself highly honored by the action you have taken on the occasion of my eighty-fourth birthday. Among the hundreds of congratulatory letters which have reached me none have been more welcome than that which comes from my native place and from the legal representatives of " mine own people."

With sincere wishes for the welfare and continued prosperity of my old home, and with grateful appreciation of your generous action,

I am your friend,

JOHN G. WHITTIER.

www.ingramcontent.com/pod-product-compliance
Lightning Source LLC
Chambersburg PA
CBHW032112010726
47493CB00008B/2558